FALLING FOR A TEXAS HELLION
Previously published in: When Things Got Hot in Texas
anthology

Copyright © June 2017 by Katie Lane

Cover by The Killion Group www.thekilliongroupinc.com

Couple photography by Katie Lane

Printed in the USA.

Cover Design and Interior Format

Falling for a

TEXAS
HELLION

A TENDER HEART TEXAS NOVEL

KATIE LANE

"It was easy for Lance Butler to pick out the floozy in the group of mail-order brides. The redhead not only wore a dress that showed half her bosom, she was also brazen. When she caught him staring, she smiled seductively. 'See something you like, Cowboy?'"

~Tender Heart, Book Five

ℭ

CHAPTER ONE

SOMEONE WAS IN THE HOUSE.

Mason Granger listened as the floorboards in the hallway creaked. If he were at his home in Austin, he would already have his gun in hand and pointed at the door. But he wasn't in Austin. He was in a Bliss, Texas. And the only weapon he'd brought with him was his hunting rifle.

Which was still out in his truck.

Damn.

He eased up off the bed, hoping that the old springs in the mattress would keep their silence. Once his feet were on the floor, he wasted no time moving to the wall next to the door. He might not have a weapon, but he had surprise on his side. He held his breath and waited. Another creak sounded. This one was much closer. Only a second later, a shadowy form entered the room. Mason didn't hesitate to pounce.

His intention was to tackle the invader to the floor and beat him senseless. But once his arms closed around the soft body of a woman, instinct kicked in, and he twisted to take most of the impact. He landed on the shoulder he'd injured playing college football. That injury had ended his pro sports career before it began and turned his path towards law.

"Sonofabitch!" He rolled onto his back in pain but refused to release the intruder, even though she was fighting like a hellcat. A hellcat that he remembered tussling with before. He remembered the small breasts that brushed his forearm. He remembered the long legs that tangled with his. And he remembered the shapely ass that bumped against him in a rhythm that sent a shaft of sexual awareness spearing through him. He had no business being sexually aroused by this woman. Not only because she was the younger sister of a friend, but also because he liked his women submissive. And there was nothing submissive about Becky Arrington.

"Enough, Rebecca!"

He didn't know if it was the command in his voice or the fact that he knew her identity that made Becky hold still. Probably the latter. She didn't seem like the type of woman who took commands. She released an exasperated huff as her body relaxed against his.

"I thought you were in Austin," she grumbled. "I thought that's why you couldn't be at my brother's wedding."

It was the excuse he'd given Zane so as not to hurt his friend's feelings, but the truth was that he didn't attend weddings. Any weddings. As a divorce lawyer, he dealt with too many broken vows to think of a marriage ceremony as anything more than a farce perpetuated by starry-eyed lovers with no clue about the reality of married life.

He lifted Becky and plopped her none too gently on the floor before he got to his feet. He switched on the lamp, not caring that he didn't have on a stitch of clothing. She walked into his house unannounced, she deserved to be embarrassed. He should've known better. Becky didn't even blink when he turned around. She sat on the floor with her dress hiked up and her panties showing, staring brazenly. The dress surprised him. He'd only seen her in western shirts and wrangler jeans. But the lacy pink panties surprised him even more. He hadn't taken her for a pink lace kind of girl. She was more the boy shorts type.

"You sleep naked?" she asked.

He walked over and grabbed the boxer briefs he'd stripped off earlier. "Only when it's the hottest summer in Texas history and there's no air conditioning." He pulled on the briefs and turned to find her deep blue eyes filled with annoyance.

"If my house is too hot, then maybe you should leave," Becky replied.

He moved to the window, but there wasn't a trace of breeze to cool him. The night air was thick and humid. It was also peaceful. In the city, all he could hear at night through his open windows were the harsh sounds of traffic, downtown partiers, and sirens. All he could hear now were the soothing sounds of chirping insects and the occasional hoot of an owl.

Mason needed soothing. In the last few months he'd felt restless and uneasy. He no longer got satisfaction from punishing greedy spouses in the courtroom. Nor did he get satisfaction from punishing submissive women in bed. His discontentment had prompted him to take a leave of absence from work. Foolishness had him believing that Bliss held the key to his cure.

"Your house?" he said without turning around. "Funny, I believe I'm the one who holds the deed to the house and land."

She jumped up and came striding over to stand behind him. Unlike most women, her scent wasn't manufactured perfumes or lotions. She smelled earthy . . . like fresh-cut grass on a cool spring morning.

"Only because Mr. Reed reneged on our deal when you sneaked in and offered him cash," she snapped.

He turned and raised an eyebrow. "You had a contract with Delbert Reed to buy this place?"

"Not a contract exactly. But I told him I wanted to buy it, and I would've as soon as I turned twenty-five and got my trust fund. I had plans for this ranch." She stepped closer and pointed at finger at his chest. "Plans that I'm not going to let some uppity lawyer from Austin ruin just because he wants a place to hunt and fish on the weekends."

"Is that why you snuck into my house?" He arched an eyebrow. "You planned to murder me in my sleep so you could buy the ranch from my beneficiary? I should warn you that I don't have a will so it could take some time for my estate to work its way through probate."

She sent him a smug look. "A lawyer without a will? Isn't that like a doctor without health insurance?"

He couldn't help but laugh. She might be a brat, but she was entertaining. "My life has always been tumultuous. Why not my death? But we digress. Why did you sneak into *my* house?"

Her eyes flashed with temper. He had thought they were the same blue as her brother Zane's, but on closer examination, they weren't as dark. Rays of sapphire shone through the twilight irises. "I didn't sneak. I thought you hadn't moved in yet and I came to get my . . . stuff."

"Why would your stuff be here?"

She paused before she answered. It was a tactic he'd seen often in the courtroom—usually when someone was about to lie. "Because my cousin Gracie and I used to hang out here when we were teenagers, and we left a few things behind." Her gaze flickered to the corner of the room for a brief second. From what he could tell, there was nothing there but a few cobwebs and some dust. Which made him extremely curious.

"All the furniture and household items were included in the sale," he said. "But I wouldn't want to keep anything that belongs to Zane's sister." He crossed his arms. "So please help yourself."

Becky paused again, and her gaze returned to the corner just long enough to make him even more curious. "All I want is my grandma's quilt." She grabbed the quilt off the bed. He would've bet money that it wasn't her grandma's. Especially when she looked so annoyed to have it in her possession. "Well, thanks for the stimulating conversation, Mr. Granger. And the even more stimulating peep show."

He bit back a smile. "I'm glad you enjoyed it." He followed her out, simply because he didn't trust her as far as he could throw her. With her temper, he wouldn't be surprised if she torched the place just so he wouldn't have it.

He expected to find her candy-apple-red truck parked in front of the house. Instead, a white stallion was tied to the porch railing. The horse tossed his head and snorted when they came out the door.

"You're still riding that demonic horse?" he asked.

She grabbed her boots that were sitting on the porch and sat on the steps to tug them on, which pretty much proved that she had been sneaking into his house.

"Ghost Rider is not demonic," she said. "He's just high spirited." She got up and rolled the quilt tightly before securing it to the back of the saddle. The horse pranced and jerked at the reins, confirming Mason's assessment. And even though he felt Becky needed a tough lesson on the dangers of misjudging an animal, he untied the reins from the rail and took the horse's bridle to hold him steady.

"A high-spirited horse that would've trampled you to death that day in the barn if I hadn't pushed you out of the way."

"More like tackled me. You seem to enjoy manhandling woman." She jerked the reins from him and swung into the saddle.

There was something about the image of her astride the white stallion that momentarily took his breath away. Her long golden brown hair hung almost to the horse's rump, and her aqua dress was hiked up so far he could see a hint of lacy panties and a whole lot of toned, long leg. Unable to stop himself, he took her calf and guided her boot into the stirrup before he lifted his gaze to hers.

"I only manhandle the ones who step into my lair." He slid his hand up her calf. "Fair warning, Rebecca. Next time you come into *my* home uninvited, I won't be so nice." He brushed the soft skin behind her knee with his thumb before he released her.

"I don't think you have a nice bone in your body." She whirled the horse, forcing him to jump back or get his bare feet crushed beneath its hooves, before she galloped off into the darkness. When she was gone, he released his breath and gave himself a mental warning. *Be careful, Mason. That one's not for you.*

He turned back to the house. It wasn't a pretty place. The roof needed repairs, the front porch sagged, and the trim needed sanding and painting. Not to mention the broken air conditioner. But he hadn't bought the ranch for the house. He'd bought it for its location. And it had nothing to do with fishing and hunting. The same way Becky hadn't come for her grandmother's quilt.

He walked to his Range Rover and got his rifle. He didn't expect any more visitors, but he always believed in being prepared. Back in the bedroom, he set the rifle on the bed and walked to the corner. Just as he'd suspected, there were only dust and cobwebs . . . and one loose floorboard.

Getting a knife from the kitchen, he came back and popped up the loose board. The space beneath was too dark to see anything so he had to move the lamp closer. In between the floor joists there was a small wooden box. He leaned down and pulled it out.

When he opened it, he discovered the real reason Becky had snuck into his house.

"The cowboy was tall, dark, and so handsome that Valentine momentarily lost her breath. It came back in a hurry when he spoke. 'I'm looking for a wife, not a saloon girl.'"

❦

CHAPTER TWO

BECKY TRIED TO KEEP THE image of Mason's hard, naked body from popping into her head, but it was like trying not to cuss when you stubbed your pinkie toe. Whenever she closed her eyes, each bulging muscle flickered through her brain like pornographic flash cards: broad shoulders, defined pecs, knotted biceps, ripped abs, impressive . . .

"He just moved in and was sleeping there without one stitch of clothing?" Gracie cut in as if reading her thoughts. It wasn't unusual. Becky and her cousin were as close as sisters and could always read each other's minds. Even when they were hundreds of miles apart. "Did you see his manly staff?"

Becky rolled her eyes at her cellphone, which sat on the kitchen counter. "I don't know what historical romance novel you got that name for a man's penis out of, but you need to never read it again." She poured the ground coffee into the coffeemaker.

Usually, Carly made the morning coffee . . . and a delicious breakfast to go with it. But she'd left early that morning with Zane. They would be gone for two weeks on their honeymoon in Hawaii, leaving Becky in charge of the ranch. She was more than a little excited about the prospect of running things without her big brother looking over her shoulder. But she was bummed she had to make her own coffee and cook her own meals. She had always preferred a barn to a kitchen.

"I like staff better than penis," Gracie said. "It sounds more masculine. So does this Mason have a big one or not?"

"It looked pretty big to me, but I'm not exactly an expert. It's pathetic to be almost twenty-five and still a virgin."

"I don't think it's pathetic."

"Because you're only a few years away from being in the same freak boat." She got a mug from the cupboard. "We should've had sex with the Jefferson twins when we had the chance."

"I'm not going to give my virginity to someone with bad manners and a goatee. Especially if I don't love him," Gracie said adamantly. "I don't care if it makes me a freak. I'm waiting for my Honey Bee."

Honey Bee was the reason Becky and Gracie were still virgins. If they had never found their great-aunt's diary, they never would've had such high expectations for a lover. But they did find it.

The vacant Reed property had been a perfect teenage hideout from annoying older brothers.

Becky and Gracie had filled it with old furniture and dishes and treated it like their own grown up playhouse. When they'd moved the old brass bed—the only piece of furniture left in the house by the previous tenant—closer to the window, they had discovered the loose floorboard and their great-aunt's account of her secret love affair.

Lucy Arrington was famous for writing the classic western series Tender Heart. She had written the ten book series in the 1960s and based it on the cowboys who had tamed Texas and the mail-order brides who had tamed them. Becky and Gracie grew up reading the books. They loved the stories and were completely intrigued by their aunt. Like everyone else, they thought Lucy was an eccentric old maid who never married—never even had a boyfriend. But when Becky and Gracie stumbled upon the diary, they discovered that their aunt had indeed had a boyfriend. And not just a boyfriend, but a lover.

While Lucy's books only had a few passionate kisses, her diary was filled with steamy details of the time she spent with the man she referred to as Honey Bee. The diary never said where she met the man for their sexual romps. Since they'd found the journal in the Reed House, they thought maybe that was where Lucy had met her secret lover.

If the diary had been dated, Becky and Gracie might've been able to figure out who had been living in the house at the time. But there were no dates on the diary pages, and numerous renters had lived in the house after the Reed family moved to their bigger ranch near Austin in the late 1940s.

Gracie and Becky weren't as concerned with Honey Bee as they were about guarding Lucy's secret. After reading the diary, they felt a connection to their aunt and wanted to be sure her name was not dragged through the mud. Besides, it was extremely cool to know something no one else did. The cousins would do whatever it took to keep it that way, which was exactly why Becky had snuck into the Reed house.

"Speaking of Honey Bee," she said. "We need to get back to figuring out how we're going to get the diary out of the house before Mason finds it. Obviously, sneaking in while he's sleeping isn't going to work."

"That was your idea, not mine," Gracie said. "I wanted you to just tell him it was yours and ask for it. You've always been able to flirt anything out of a guy."

She poured a cup of coffee. "Not Mason. He seems to be immune to my charms. In fact, I get the feeling that he likes me as much as I like him. If I told him the diary was mine, he'd probably sell it to the Austin newspaper. And we can't have him doing that with Lucy's diary."

"You're right." Gracie paused. "But I don't think we should move the diary either. Lucy left it there as a tribute to what she shared with Honey Bee. Taking it from the house would be like taking flowers from a grave."

"So you just want to let Mason have it?"

"Of course not. I don't want him to have the diary or the house. That house is where Lucy found her Tender Heart. Where she learned about love so she could write about it in her books."

Gracie had always been such a romantic, while Becky dealt more in reality. "I don't know if I'd go that far. If she'd found love, why didn't they ever get married?"

"Maybe something tragic happened," Gracie said. "Maybe Honey Bee died before they could get married."

"Or maybe it was just hot sex."

Gracie gasped, but Becky didn't see anything wrong with that. She didn't want to get married. She'd spent her entire life with a bossy daddy and brother. She didn't need to add a bossy husband to the mix. And if she was going to be like Lucy Arrington and never get married, she had decided to get her own Honey Bee. A Honey Bee who would satisfy her at night but stay out of her business during the day.

But finding the right bee for the job hadn't been easy. Becky had dated dozens of guys in the last year and not one had made her want to get her flower pollinated. And some, like Rich Myers, had made her want to grab a can of hornet spray.

"How can you say that, Becky?" Gracie asked. "You've read the diary. You know how much Lucy loved him. And it's up to us to keep that love a secret. I truly believe that Lucy wanted us to find the diary. Just like she wanted me to find the first chapter of the final book of the Tender Heart series so Cole and Emery could live happily ever after."

While Becky didn't believe in fate, it did seem like more than a coincidence that Gracie had found the first chapter. Lucy had died before publishing the final book, and after her death, her relatives had searched high and low for the manuscript. Decades later, Gracie had found a long-lost chapter in the floor of the little white chapel. Becky couldn't deny that the chapter had brought Emery to Bliss and subsequently into Cole's arms. But it also might have contributed to the accident that had put Gracie in a wheelchair. If she hadn't been in such a hurry to get back and tell her father and brother about finding the chapter, she might not have been thrown from her horse. And instead of being at a rehabilitation center in Dallas, she would be at home with her cousin.

"So how are we going to get rid of Mason and get our house back?" Becky asked.

There was a long silence, and Becky knew Gracie's mind was working. Most folks thought she was as sweet as spring rain, but her cousin had a devious side. This was proven when she spoke.

"You told me he's a lawyer who bought the property as a vacation home. And the only reason a big city man would buy a piece of land in the middle of nowhere is for peace and quiet. I say we give him just the opposite."

Becky almost spit out the sip of coffee she'd just taken. "Are we talking chaos and noise?"

"Exactly." She could almost see Gracie's evil smile. "Why don't you call Ms. Marble and see if she can notify the welcoming committee. I bet Mr. Granger would love folks dropping by to welcome him. And doesn't the roof on the Reed house need a little work? I think it would be real neighborly of you to send some ranch hands over to fix it. Oh, and make sure they take big hammers."

Becky laughed. "Why, Gracie Lynn Arrington, you little devil."

"I'm just wanting to make sure the man feels welcome, is all. And make sure to call Winnie Crawley. Once she sinks her nails into a guy, he can't get away fast enough."

For some reason, Becky didn't like the idea of Winnie sinking her nails into Mason. Probably because she couldn't stand the thought of all that perfection being marred. But if she wanted to get rid of him, Winnie was the fastest way to do it. And she did want to get rid of him. She didn't care as much about the house or Lucy's diary as Gracie did, but she did care about the land.

Most people viewed the Reed property as too small to raise a large herd of cattle, but Becky had been reading up on rotational grazing where you need less land to feed more cattle. She had talked to Zane about trying it on the Earhart Ranch, but he was too set in his ways. For him to try it, he'd need proof that it worked. Becky wanted to give him that proof by turning the Reed property into a successful ranch.

"Okay," she said. "Let's make Mason's life hell. Then in a few weeks, when I turn twenty-five and get my trust fund, I'll make him an offer he can't—"

The doorbell cut her off. It was only a little after six o'clock in the morning, but on a working ranch everyone was up at the crack of dawn.

"I've got to go," she said as she set down her cup of coffee. "I'll call you later." She hung up the phone and headed for the door. But when she opened it there was no one there. She stepped out onto the porch and looked around. The sun was just breaking over the horizon, casting the yard in a pinkish glow. A rooster crowed in the distance, and their herding dog Shep barked to be let out of the barn. But there were no ranch hands around or trucks parked next to hers.

She started to go back inside when she noticed her truck and froze. A huge teddy bear sat behind the steering wheel, its beady black eyes staring sightlessly back at her. While plenty of girls would love a stuffed animal surprise from a secret admirer, Becky didn't. Mostly because the admirer's identity wasn't a secret.

Rich Myers had been a ranch hand Zane hired last fall. He was handsome, mannerly, and charming, which is why Becky had considered him a potential Honey Bee. But as soon as he got her alone, his charm and manners had flown right out his truck window. He'd turned into an overbearing jerk who wouldn't take no for an answer.

It had taken a hard knee to the groin to get him to release her. When Zane found out she'd walked home after their date, he'd fired Rich the next day and sent him packing. She thought that would be the last of the man. But he had turned out to be persistent. He continued to ask her out with flowers and gifts. At first it was just annoying. But recently, it had started feeling kind of creepy to find her truck filled with flowers, stuffed animals, and love poems pieced together with words clipped out of a magazine like a kidnapper's random note. And Becky didn't like feeling scared. She didn't like it at all.

Since Rich couldn't have run off that quickly after ringing the doorbell, she figured he was hiding somewhere nearby. She went down the porch steps and jerked opened the door of her truck. The teddy bear toppled right out at her boots. She didn't pick it up. Instead, she stomped the shit out of it, ripping a hole in its nose and cracking both plastic eyes. And when the thing looked like it had been violently assaulted at the teddy bear picnic, she kicked it into the middle of the road.

"Listen up, Rich," she yelled. "If you don't leave me alone, I'm going to do the same thing to you that I did to this bear. Now get off my property before I call the sheriff!"

"Being elected the mayor of Tender Heart had put Lance in a bad position. All the mail-order brides' complaints about food, lodging, and horny cowboys landed on his doorstep . . . via the redhead with the big breasts and even bigger mouth."

☾

CHAPTER THREE

WHEN MASON HAD PULLED BECKY'S diary from the box, he'd expected to find a young girl's ramblings about boys and sweet prom kisses. He had not expected a steamy pornographic journal of the sex she was having with some guy named Honey Bee.

The journal explained why Becky wanted the house. She didn't want to lose the place where she had her secret rendezvous. Mason found that puzzling. Why did she keep her affair a secret? Not only was the prose steamy, it also rambled on and on about her love for the guy. If she loved him, why didn't she date him openly? There was only one answer he could think of.

Honey Bee was already married.

As a divorce lawyer, Mason had seen it time and time again. A husband having a secret affair because he had no intention of leaving his wife. It was more than likely that Honey Bee was just using Becky.

A meow pulled his attention from the diary. A mangy-looking cat sat on the end of the porch. Its gray fur was matted and one of its ears looked like it had been chewed off. Mason didn't know a lot about cats, or dogs for that matter. His mother had been allergic to animal dander, so he hadn't had pets as a kid. And now he was too busy to deal with a pet. But if the skinny body and desperate look were any indication, this cat was starving.

He got up and walked inside. He had gone into town earlier and stocked up on groceries. He pulled some deli turkey out of the refrigerator. As he was placing a couple slices on a paper plate, the ornate urn on the windowsill caught his eye.

The kitchen probably wasn't the best place for his mother's ashes. But he didn't want them in his bedroom, and there was no furniture in the living area or the other bedroom. So unless he wanted to put the urn on the back of the toilet, the kitchen was the only place left. Besides, cooking was one of the few things his mother had enjoyed doing.

That, and reading Tender Heart novels.

As soon as he set the paper plate on the porch, the cat dove into the turkey, holding the plate with its paw as it licked it clean. Since it was so hot out, Mason went back inside and got a bowl of water. He issued a warning as he set it down next to the plate. "This is a one-shot deal. I don't want a cat."

The cat lapped some water before it shot him a disdainful look and curled up on the porch. Mason was considering running the animal off when an Oldsmobile came up the road. The Oldsmobile appeared to be driven by a big Easter bonnet. It came to a dust-spitting stop in front of the porch, and a little old woman got out.

"Goodness, it's hotter than Hell's pepper patch today." She patted her forehead with a white-gloved hand before she opened the back door of the car and pulled out a basket that was almost as big as she was. Being from Texas, he knew a welcome basket when he saw one. While he had no desire to become chummy with his neighbors, he couldn't exactly ignore a sweet-looking little old lady.

He quickly came down the porch steps. "Let me get that, ma'am."

She handed the basket over, then gave him a thorough once-over that had him feeling embarrassed about not having a shirt on.

"Well, no wonder Becky wants to make sure you feel welcome," she said. "You look like Cary Grant on steroids."

Becky? Now why would Becky want to welcome him when she wanted him out of her love nest as soon as possible? Obviously, she was up to something. He glanced at the brownies inside the basket. Had she baked him poison brownies and talked this innocent little old woman into delivering them? He wouldn't put it past her.

The woman held out her white-gloved hand. "Maybelline Marble. School teacher for close to forty years and now the baker for Lucy's Place Diner."

"Mason Granger." Mason took her hand expecting a gentle squeeze. Instead, he got a firm shake.

"An excellent attorney from what I hear." When he lifted an eyebrow in question, she shrugged her thin shoulders. "I Googled you. It always pays to have a little information on the new people who come to town. We don't want any riffraff, but we certainly could use a good cutthroat attorney."

Mason took a closer look at the woman. She might be elderly and petite, but there was a sharpness in her steely blue eyes that made him realize she wasn't a woman to underestimate.

"I don't usually go for the throat as much as the wallet," he said dryly.

She tipped back her head and laughed. "I do love a man who doesn't beat around the bush." She hooked her arm through his. "Now let's go inside and get out of this blasted heat. I have a few questions about my will I need answered."

Since he couldn't be disrespectful, he led the woman up the steps of the front porch. He picked up the diary out of the chair on the way past. The woman's direct gaze landed on the book briefly before moving to the cat.

"A cat man. How sweet."

Mason was going to deny being a cat man and sweet, but then chose to ignore the comment. He held open the door. "Sorry that it's not much cooler inside. My air conditioner isn't working."

Ms. Marble released his arm and moved into the living room. "To be honest, I wasn't really worried about the heat. I just wanted to see the inside of the house once again."

"Once again?"

She turned back to him. "I lived here right after

I married my first husband." She got a far-off look in her eyes. "The Reeds let us live here for free because Justin had served in the military." She smiled. "Lord, times were tough back then. I was a new teacher and working at the diner at night until Justin could find a job. But I didn't mind. I was in love."

She flapped a gloved hand. "But look at me going on like a love-struck ninny." She took the basket from him and headed to the kitchen where she proceeded to pull out a thickly wrapped plate of brownies and a mason jar of what looked like sweet tea.

Mason didn't drink tea, sweet or otherwise, but Ms. Marble wasn't a woman you refused. While she got everything ready, he went into the bedroom to get a shirt. He shoved the diary under his pillow. He should put it back in the floor. And he would. Once he finished reading it.

When he stepped out of the bedroom, Ms. Marble was placing two glasses of tea on the scarred kitchen table. She had removed her gloves and hat, and her white hair resembled a flattened dandelion puff. There was something about her tottering around his dingy little kitchen that made him happy and sad at the same time. He didn't know either of his grandmothers. His parents had divorced when he was only two and he didn't have a relationship with his father's side of the family. And his mother's mom had died before he was born.

Ms. Marble glanced up and noticed him standing in the doorway of the bedroom and smiled. "Well, don't just stand there dawdling. The ice in your sweet tea will melt." He walked over and pulled out her chair. Her smile got even bigger. "Your mama taught you well."

He couldn't help but glance at the urn. When he noticed Ms. Marble watching him, he quickly took the chair opposite her. "She didn't care what else I did, but she was a stickler for manners." He didn't know why he had confided in Ms. Marble. His past wasn't something he shared. Mostly because he hated sympathy.

Surprisingly, Ms. Marble didn't give him any. She studied him for a long moment with those steely eyes before she picked up the plate. "Brownie?"

If the woman was in cahoots with Becky and the brownies were poisoned, he'd die happy. The chocolaty dessert was the best thing he'd tasted in a long time. He polished off one and then moved to a second while he answered all of Ms. Marble's questions about her will. He had heard about chocolate releasing endorphins, but he hadn't believed it until now. For the first time in a long time, he felt content as he settled back in his chair.

"Who is putting your will together?" he asked. "Zane?"

"Zane is much too busy ranching to practice law. And since we don't have another lawyer in Bliss, I had to get one from Austin. But I have to tell you that I don't like the man. He treats me like I'm two steps away from the grave." She sent him a sideways glance. "How long do you plan on being here in Bliss?"

"I'm not sure," he said. "But I'll be happy to help you with your will while I'm here." He nodded at the brownies. "As long as you bring me more of those."

She smiled. "Just wait until you taste my cinnamon swirl muffins. I would've brought you some, but I took most of them to the diner and the rest to Becky. With Carly and Zane gone on their honeymoon, that girl will be so wrapped up in ranch work she'll forget to eat."

Or wrapped up in her Honey Bee.

"So, is Becky dating anyone?" Mason asked.

He realized his mistake when her eyes immediately started to twinkle. "Becky dates a lot, but no one man has caught her eye for any length of time." She sent him a knowing look. "Of course, I have a feeling that's about to change." Before he could discourage any thoughts of him and Becky, she continued. "And not a moment too soon. She needs a boyfriend to get rid of that scoundrel Rich Myers for her."

He couldn't help wondering if this Rich was Becky's Honey Bee. "Why is he a scoundrel? Is he married?"

Ms. Marble took a sip of her tea. "I wouldn't doubt it. I tried Googling him, but there are way too many Richard Myers. Still, I don't have to research him online to know a stalker when I see one. He's been following Becky around like a stray dog after dinner scraps since he's come to town."

If he was Becky's Honey Bee, she'd given him more than scraps. "Maybe Becky likes him."

"That's doubtful. Especially after what I saw this morning."

He cringed. He certainly hoped the sweet little

woman hadn't witnessed some of the things he'd read about in the diary.

"When I pulled up to the ranch this morning to deliver the muffins," she continued, "there was a huge pile of stuffing and fur right in the middle of the road. I got out to investigate and found a ripped-up teddy bear with a note attached to the ribbon around its neck." She lifted her almost invisible eyebrows. "'You can't ignore me forever. You're mine. Rich.' Now if that's not a stalker's note, I don't know what is. And if I'd received it, I would've done exactly what Becky did. I would've ripped that thing to shreds and tossed it in the road."

Obviously, Rich wasn't Honey Bee . . . unless they had gotten into some kind of lover's quarrel. It was possible with Becky. That woman could provoke a saint.

"I wouldn't worry too much about it," he said. "It sounds like Becky can take care of herself."

"That's what she wants people to believe, but every woman needs help now and—" An overhead thumping had her looking at the ceiling. "What in the world?"

Mason got to his feet and headed for the door. Outside, he stepped over the sleeping cat on the porch and moved down the steps. Two men crouched on his roof with sagging tool belts. "Can I help you?" he called up to them.

One of the men got to his feet and moved closer to the edge of the roof. "Miss Becky sent us over from the Earhart Ranch to fix your roof. It shouldn't take us more than a couple days. Three tops."

"I don't want my roof—" The other man starting hammering and drowned Mason out. Exasperated, he headed for the ladder propped on the side of the house. But before he could reach it, a car came barreling up the drive and stopped in a cloud of dust. A young woman jumped out. She wore more makeup than a televangelist's wife, but there was nothing holy about her skintight top and short shorts.

"Well, Becky certainly wasn't lying when she said you were hot." She ran her tongue over her brightly painted lips. "You're sizzlin'."

"It had become Valentine's amusing pastime to see just how annoyed she could make the mayor of Tender Heart."

❦

CHAPTER FOUR

"I CAN'T BELIEVE YOU SET WINNIE Crawley on that unsuspecting dude." Dirk Hadley flipped a hamburger on the cooktop and pressed it down with the back of his spatula. "I've been on the receiving end of Winnie's desire, and believe me, it's not fun."

Becky sat on a barstool at the prep counter and munched on a crispy French fry. Since it was after the lunch rush, no one was in the diner except her and Dirk. "Tell that to someone who doesn't know you. You love being the subject of a woman's desires."

Dirk shot a sexy smile over his shoulder. And the man had one sexy smile. He would make a great Honey Bee. He was smoking hot and had no desire to get married. It was too bad Becky wasn't interested in his stinger. An image of Mason's stinger popped into her head—something that happened a lot lately. But he was not a Honey Bee. He was a snake. A poisonous snake that she needed to stay away from.

"If you and Gracie wanted the property so badly, why didn't y'all buy it sooner?" Dirk asked. He spoke with an East Texas twang. Although no one was sure where he came from or what he was doing here in Bliss. He'd just shown up a few months back and started doing odd jobs for the townsfolk. With his devilish charm and ability to do any job well, he quickly became a town favorite. He had worked for Cole on his ranch, Zane and Becky on theirs, and now worked as a short-order cook at Lucy's Place diner. He had been a darn good rancher and was just as good a cook.

Becky dabbed another French fry in catsup and polished it off. "Because I have a daddy who thinks if I get too much money before I outgrow my wild streak I'll spend it on high-strung horses, fast motorcycles, and rundown ranches. All my profits go back into the ranch or into a trust fund that I won't get until I'm twenty-five."

Dirk laughed. "Smart daddy."

"More like controlling daddy. He still sees me as his little girl who can't wipe her nose without his or Zane's help. Which is exactly why I want my own ranch. I'm tired of never being consulted when they make decisions about the ranch. With my own ranch, I'll be the boss." She tapped her chest. "I'll make the decisions."

"But why does it have to be the Reed place? You'll be twenty-five soon. Why don't you just buy another piece of land to ranch?"

She hesitated for only a second. With Gracie in Dallas, Dirk had become her confidant and friend. She trusted him and felt comfortable letting him in on her and Gracie's secret. "If I tell you, you have to promise not to tell a soul."

Dirk turned from the stove and handed her a plate with a cheeseburger on it. "Let me guess. This has to do with the final Tender Heart book. You found another chapter. It seems everyone in town is looking for that book."

It was the truth. The entire town had been searching for more chapters since Gracie had found the first one. As far as Becky knew, another one hadn't turned up. "No. But it does have to do with Lucy Arrington." She dug into the cheeseburger, which was cooked a perfect medium, while Dirk turned back to the stove and started scraping off the charred burger remains with his spatula.

After a while, he asked, "What about Lucy?"

Becky chewed and swallowed. "She had a lover. A lover she used to meet in the Reed house."

Since he hadn't grown up in Bliss and had never shown any interest in the series, she didn't expect him to be overly excited. But she didn't expect him to be angry either. But that's exactly how he looked when he stopped scraping and turned. His easygoing smile was gone and his pretty gray eyes were narrowed. Obviously, he was a bigger Tender Heart fan than she'd thought and didn't like the idea of Lucy being anything but pure.

"And what makes you think that Lucy met her lover in the Reed house?"

"Gracie and I found her diary in the floor of the house, and it's filled with stories about her lover Honey Bee. Which means that the house is a historical landmark. It shouldn't belong to a man who probably hasn't even picked up a Tender Heart book. It should belong to one of Lucy's relatives."

Dirk's eyebrows lifted. "You."

"And Gracie." She took another big bite of burger.

"Except Gracie really isn't an Arrington by blood."

Becky wasn't surprised he knew about Gracie being adopted. He and Gracie had gotten close before she left. "It doesn't matter. She loves the Tender Heart series more than anyone."

"Have you talked to her since she started therapy? How's it going?"

"I talk with her daily, but she refuses to tell me how her therapy is going. She even asked her doctors and therapists to keep her progress from Cole, which leads me to believe that it's not going well."

Dirk stared down at his scuffed cowboy boots. "Damn. I had hoped . . ." He let the sentence drift off.

No longer hungry, Becky set her cheeseburger down. "We've all hoped that she would walk again. But it doesn't look like that's going to happen, and Gracie must be crushed. Before the accident, she was so independent. I know she hates the thought of coming back and being a burden to her brother. Especially now that he's married to Emery." She rested her chin in her hand and heaved a sigh. "I thought that if I could buy the Reed place and give her something to come back to that it might make her feel like less of a burden. Like she had a purpose. I really believe we can turn that place into a great ranch."

Dirk glanced up, and he got a resigned look in his eyes. "Fine. How can I help you get rid of the guy?'

*

After finishing lunch, Becky headed back to the ranch. She needed to check the pond in the south pasture. With the heat wave, water levels were dropping rapidly, and she might have to move the herd to the north pasture where there was more water. If the drought kept up, they'd have to pipe in water from the municipal system. She prayed it would rain soon.

The scrolled iron entrance to the Earhart Ranch always made her feel proud. She liked that the ranch was named after the one in the Tender Heart series. The original Arrington Ranch had covered thousands of acres, but her father and his two brothers had gotten in an argument about how the ranch should be run. When they couldn't solve their differences, they split the ranch up three ways. Her cousin Cole's father had kept the name Arrington for his ranch. Her cousin Raff's father had chosen Tender Heart for his ranch's name. And Becky and Zane's dad had chosen Earhart.

As soon as she drove onto the ranch, her cell-phone rang. She glanced at the screen on her dash and rolled her eyes. She loved her mama, but talking to Misty Arrington was like talking to an alien from another planet. She and Becky were complete opposites. Misty loved all things girlie. She especially loved planning parties. Now that Zane and Carly's wedding was over, she was ready to move on to her daughter's twenty-fifth birthday party. She usually did a surprise party for Becky. But this year, she had decided to bring Becky in on the planning. Which was suspicious . . . and painful.

"I'm thinking pink," her mama's excited voice came out of the truck speakers as soon as Becky answered. "Pink flowers. Pink tablecloths. Those pretty pink puff balls that hang from the ceiling— did you get the pink bra and panty set I sent you, honey?"

"Yes, mama. I got it. And the other twenty sets you sent me too."

"Good. You'll need pretty lingerie when you get married. It's not easy pulling a rancher's attention away from his cows."

Becky didn't mention the fact that she wasn't getting married. She didn't want her mama to have a heart attack. She had started planning her only daughter's wedding from the moment Becky slipped out of the birth canal.

"Now what about food?" her mother continued. "Your brother insisted on barbecue for his wedding reception, but I think that's much too messy for a young woman's birthday. I'm thinking more of a nice seared salmon."

Becky hated salmon as much as she hated pink. Okay, so maybe she didn't hate all pink. The lingerie her mama had sent her was pretty. "Whatever you think is good, Mama. I'll leave it all up to you."

"Then we'll do fish. I already booked a hotel ballroom here in Austin and I'll get that string quartet that played for your brother's wedding. I know how much you love classical music." *Not.* "And don't forget that you need to leave bright and early on Saturday morning," her mama continued. "We'll need to go shopping for your dress and shoes, then you have your hair, nail, and tanning appointments before your party that night."

Becky stared up at the roof of her truck. Good Lord. She thought birthdays were supposed to be about what you wanted. Not about what your mama did. But she kept her mouth shut. All she cared about was getting her trust fund so she could buy out Mason and get her ranch.

Her mama continued to talk about the party plans, but Becky stopped listening when a faint bawling drew her attention. She stopped the truck and rolled down both windows. The bawling grew louder, but it was hard to figure out what direction it came from with her mama's non-stop chatter.

"Listen, Mama, I need to call you back," she said.

"You'd better, young lady. Last time you said that, I didn't hear from you until the following day."

"I promise. Love you." Becky hung up.

The bawling continued, and she drove slowly along the road until she reached a point where it was the loudest. It was definitely a baby calf that had gotten lost from its mama or found itself in some other trouble. It didn't make any sense. They didn't keep cattle this close to the house.

She turned off the road and headed across the field. It didn't take her long to spot the Angus calf.

It was tangled in a barbed wire fence. She stopped the truck only feet away, grabbed her gloves, then hopped out and got the wire cutters from the toolbox in the bed of the truck.

When she reached the calf, he was struggling so much that she had to go back to the truck and get her rope. She quickly straddled him and tied his legs. When he was lying motionless, she realized he was bleeding badly and not from the barbed wire gouges as much as the deep cut on his hip.

A cut in the shape of an X right over the heart-encircled E of the Earhart brand.

"All Lance wanted was a relaxing day of fishing, free of mail-order brides. Instead, he stumbled upon Valentine doing her laundry in the creek."

(6

CHAPTER FIVE

BY THE TIME MASON SENT Winnie Crawley and the roofers packing and helped Ms. Marble to her car, he was fit to be tied. And if there was any tying to be done, Mason was usually the one doing it. He didn't like being manipulated, and he had little doubt that Becky had sent the townspeople to his house as part of some harebrained scheme to get rid of him. Well, it wasn't going to work. She might be able to bend other people to her will, but she wouldn't bend him. He intended to set things straight with her right now.

But finding someone on hundreds of acres of land wasn't easy. He bounced along the dirt roads of the Earhart Ranch in his Range Rover for what felt like hours before he spotted her bright-red truck.

He parked on the road and strode across the pasture to the fence she was working on. She was back in wranglers, the snug fit showing off her curvy butt. A butt his hand itched to smack. Repeatedly. But without the jeans. If he was going to spank her, he wanted nothing between her sweet, round bottom and his hand. Before he could let the fantasy unfold, he noticed the blood on her gloves and shirt. He broke into a run. When he got closer to the fence and saw the calf entangled in the barbed wire, he breathed a little easier. But he didn't like seeing an animal suffer.

"What can I do?" he asked.

She glanced over for only a second before she started issuing orders. "Hold the piece of wire so I can cut it." He knelt to do her bidding, but doing Becky's bidding wasn't easy. "Not that one," she snapped. "The one next to it." He lifted the next wire, and she efficiently snipped it. "Now move down to the next barb and hold him steady," she ordered.

The calf didn't look like it could move with its legs roped and tied, so Mason only rested a hand on its side. The calf jerked, and Becky barked, "Could you just hold him steady? I didn't take you for a weakling."

Mason was not used to being insulted. Especially by a woman who was already on his shit list. His anger simmered down deep as he followed her orders and she finished clipping the wire off. Once the calf was free, she didn't untie it. Instead, she went to pick it up. It was the final straw.

"I'll get him." Mason physically moved her out of the way before he hefted the calf into his arms. "Where to?"

"We need to get him to the ranch." Becky headed to her truck. He expected her to fold down the tailgate so he could put the cow in the bed.

Instead, she opened the passenger's side. "You'll have to hold him."

He understood why he had to hold the calf when Becky backed up and took off over the field. She drove like a maniac.

"Would you slow down!" he barked as the truck dipped into a pothole. If he wasn't wearing a cow as a seatbelt, he would've been catapulted right through the windshield.

She glanced over and grinned. "What? Does a little off-roading scare you, city boy?"

Mason gritted his teeth and kept his comments to himself as she continued to drive like she was at a monster truck rally—hitting more potholes than she missed. It was a miracle that they made it to the ranch in one piece. As soon as Becky pulled up front, she jumped out of the truck and started hollering. Ranch hands came out of the wood-work. One took the calf from Mason, another headed over to Becky.

"What happened, Miss Becky?"

"A calf got tangled in a fence in the pasture just behind the bunkhouse."

The man looked confused. "But we don't graze the herd there."

Becky ignored the statement. "Just make sure that the wounds get washed thoroughly, Jess. And call the vet if they look too deep. I'm going to wash up. I'll be out in the barn to check on him later." She turned and headed inside without one word to Mason.

No thanks for the help.

No go to hell.

No nothing.

As a partner in his law firm and as a sexual dominant, he understood giving orders. But when his orders were followed, he made sure to show gratitude. He hesitated for only a moment before he followed Becky inside.

The ranch house was so large and spread out that it took him a while to locate her bedroom. It looked just as he expected it to. No pretty lace. No girlie prints. The colors were bold and dark. The furniture was solid and massive. The bed was unmade, and there were clothes and boots scattered all over the floor. He spotted the pair of pink satin and lace panties she'd been wearing the night before. A few feet away was a matching bra. The sound of a shower pulled his attention to the closed door to the right. It wasn't locked. Obviously, no one dared interrupt Princess Becky in her bath.

He dared.

He opened the door without knocking and walked in. She was already in the shower. Her bloody clothes were piled in a corner, and behind the shower curtain she was singing a Miranda Lambert song. Badly. Her voice was off key, and she substituted words. And even though he was pissed, he couldn't help being amused as he stripped off his bloody t-shirt and tossed it in the corner with her clothes. He turned on the sink and scrubbed the blood off his hands and forearms. He had just finished toweling off when the shower stopped and the curtain slid back.

He got a glimpse of small perfect breasts with pretty rose tips and a strip of dark between toned pale thighs before she turned to grab a towel. Still, the image was seared into his brain and caused him to harden beneath the fly of his jeans. He was surprised by his reaction. He had seen a lot of naked women, much more voluptuous and sexy than Becky, but none who had got him as hard as a fourteen-year-old with his first *Playboy*.

Even after she wrapped a towel around her body, he struggled to keep his breath even and his desire from raging out of control. Maybe it was the long, toned legs that would perfectly encase a man's waist, or the soft, pale shoulders that begged for his kisses, or the lush, pink lips that opened in startled surprise when she finally turned and saw him.

"What are you doing?" She pointed a finger at the door. "Get out. Now!"

The snappish order brought back the anger that he'd been fighting since leaving his house, and mixed with the desire that pooled in his loins, he did something he never did. He moved to dominate her without any agreement between them. He backed her against the wall and clamped one hand on her trim waist. The other he fisted in her wet hair, yanking until her head snapped back and her eyes locked with his.

"There are a few things we need to get straight, Rebecca."

"For not being interested, Lance couldn't seem to keep his eyes off her. Valentine finally left her wash and sashayed over to the rock he sat on. She took the fishing pole from him. 'If you want to catch a fish, you're going about it all wrong.'"

&

CHAPTER SIX

BECKY WANTED TO YELL AT Mason for walking into her bathroom uninvited, but there was something about the way he took possession of her body that made her brain short circuit and her stomach drop. She felt like she did when she jumped a ditch on her motocross bike. She hung in midair, not knowing if she was going to land successfully or crash and burn. This time, she thought she might crash. Her body already felt like it was burning. The grip of his hand on her waist and the slightly painful tangle of his fingers in her hair kindled a fire deep down inside.

"I don't like being talked down to," he said in a low growl that brushed her forehead in chocolate-scented heat. "You want me to do something for you, you need to use the right words."

She stared into his dark eyes, trying to figure out what he was talking about. But her mind was completely numbed by all the sensations that raced through her body. "Huh?"

"When you ask me for something, I want to hear *please*. When I do it for you, I want to hear *thank you*. Do you understand?"

Most of the fogginess left her to be replaced by annoyance at Mason's arrogance. "Sorry, but I have trouble with those words," she said. "Just ask my brother and daddy."

His eyes darkened further, which she wouldn't have thought possible. They went from a deep mahogany color to a dark walnut. "I'm not your brother or your daddy."

He kissed her.

It was not the kind of kiss she was used to. She'd thought of a kiss as a soft, sweet mating of lips. But there was nothing soft or sweet about Mason's kiss. He held her hostage while his lips conquered and his tongue lay claim to her mouth. It was hot and dangerous and savage. And Becky liked it. She liked it a lot.

She put her arms around his waist and pulled him closer. The press of his hard, warm chest caused her to moan. He answered with a low, deep growl that vibrated through her body to the quivery spot between her legs. She stood on her tiptoes, pushing the aching spot against the hard fly of his jeans. But before she could get the right amount of friction, he ended the kiss. He would've pulled away if she hadn't held him tight.

"More," she breathed against his lips. "I want more."

His eyelids lowered to half-mast as he studied her mouth. "If you want something, Rebecca, you need to ask nicely."

Even with desire scrambling her brains, she knew exactly what he wanted from her. She also knew exactly what she wanted from him. "Please, give me more, Mason."

He stared at her for what felt like an eternity before his hands slid under the towel to her butt cheeks. He lifted her completely off her feet and shoved her back against the wall. Their lips met in a hard crush of moist heat. He sucked her bottom lip into his mouth, scraping his teeth along the sensitive inside before he delved deeper with a thrust of his tongue. She sucked it hard, and he moaned and squeezed her bottom, rubbing her against his erection. Then as quickly as the kiss had started, it stopped and he lowered her to the floor.

She tried to pull him back. "More please."

He peeled her hands away from his back. "No more, Rebecca. Now thank me so I can go."

With some space between her and his hot body, she could finally think. And the first thing that popped into her head was *What the heck have I done?* Followed quickly by *What an arrogant jackass.*

She glared at him and grabbed the towel that was starting to slip. "And just what would I be thanking you for? Should I thank you for barging into my bathroom without an invitation? For shoving me against the wall and pulling my hair? Or were you talking about the mediocre kiss?"

He laughed. "I think we both know there was nothing mediocre about those kisses." His gaze lowered to the arm she was using to hold the towel, and his smile dropped. "Jesus. Why didn't you tell me you were injured?"

Becky looked down. The gash she'd gotten while trying to free the calf had started bleeding again and blood dripped onto the towel. "It's just a scratch. I had the bleeding stopped until you started manhandling me."

"And I'm going to manhandle you some more." He flipped down the lid of the toilet and pulled her over to it. "Sit."

She refused. "I'm not a dog." She smiled smugly. "If you want me to do something, then you need to ask nicely."

His eyes narrowed. "Very cute. Now sit down." When she shook her head, he released an exasperated sigh and spoke through his teeth. "Please sit down, Rebecca, so I can clean your cut."

She lifted her chin. "First you need to get me my robe. I don't want you ogling my body."

He lowered his eyes, and under his gaze her nipples tightened against the towel. "It is indeed ogle worthy." The compliment went a long way toward dissolving her annoyance with him. She had to admit that he was pretty ogle worthy himself.

His jeans were snug enough to show off his package, and cut to ride low on his trim hips. A line of dark hair trailed up from the waistband, dividing the six-pack of his stomach muscles before spreading out between his hard pecs.

He hadn't shaved that morning. Sexy scruff covered his strong jaw and chin. She could see the dimple in his chin—or was it called a cleft? Whatever it was called she liked it. She also liked his wide, firm mouth and his dark, thickly lashed eyes.

If he wasn't such a jackass, she might consider making Mason her Honey Bee. Her flower was certainly drawn to his stinger, and she had little doubt that sex with him would be amazing. It just wouldn't be worth dealing with his arrogance.

He cocked a dark brow as if he knew what she was thinking. " Where is your robe?"

"On the back of the door."

He closed the door and took her robe off the hook and held it up. There was a major contrast between the forceful man who'd kissed her sense-less and the courteous gentleman who held her robe as if they were getting ready to leave on a date.

"Would you hurry up before you bleed to death?" he snapped.

Or maybe not that much of a contrast. She slipped her arms into the robe and tied it, then let the towel drop before she sat down on the toilet. "I'm not going to bleed to death. It's just a scratch from the barbed wire."

"A scratch that could easily become infected if not cleaned properly." He wet a washcloth, then knelt next to her and took her arm. He was so gentle it was almost humorous. "Have you had a tetanus shot?"

"Yes, but not my cootie one."

He glanced up. "Excuse me?"

"Don't tell me you haven't heard of a cootie shot. A cootie shot is a pinch you get from your girlfriends so boys don't give you their cooties. Didn't you learn that in elementary school?"

He got a squirt of hand soap from the dispenser

on the counter and bent closer as he rubbed it into her cut. His dark hair was mussed, and she suddenly had the strong desire to run her fingers through it and muss it even more. "I didn't go to a public elementary school with girls," he said. "I went to a private boys' school. Therefore I didn't have to worry about getting . . . cooties. Where's your antiseptic ointment?"

"Second drawer. Well, that explains why you don't know how to deal with women."

He stopped unscrewing the ointment and the look he sent her was suggestive and hot. "I've never had any complaints about the way I deal with women."

She tried to ignore the spot between her legs that still tingled. "You're way too bossy for one thing." He rubbed ointment into the cut, and the callus on his thumb made the tingling grow stronger.

"And you're not? You ordered me around with that calf like I was your whipping boy."

"I don't whip my boys. I only tie them up and spank them." She was teasing, but he didn't seem to get the joke. His gaze snapped up, and the heat in his eyes made her feel a little lightheaded. She swallowed hard. "I was kidding." He continued to stare at her until she looked away. "What are you doing here, anyway?"

He reached for the box of Band-Aids in the drawer. "I was coming to tell you to call off your minions."

"My minions?" She sent him an innocent look. "I don't know what you're talking about."

"Don't play dumb, Rebecca. It doesn't become

you. I have little doubt that Zane told you I wanted the ranch to escape the stress of my job. You figure if you disrupt my peace and quiet, I'll sell out and leave Bliss for good."

Since the jig was up, she dropped the pretense. "Which is exactly what you should do. Believe me, Bliss really isn't all that peaceful. There are much more peaceful towns. In fact, I'll even be happy to help you find one."

"I don't want to live in another town." He placed the Band-Aid on her arm and rubbed the tabs to make sure they stuck. The man had to have the hottest skin in Texas. She felt scorched.

"Why? What's so special about Bliss? Is it because Zane lives here?"

He got to his feet. "I like Zane, but it has nothing to do with him."

"Then what does it have to do with?"

"It has to do with the history."

"Of Bliss?"

He stared down at her for a moment before he spoke. "No, Tender Heart."

She couldn't have been more shocked. "You've read the books?"

He closed the box of Band-Aids and put them back in the drawer. "My mother was a devoted fan. She used to read the stories to me when I was a kid."

There went her theory of Mason not knowing a thing about the Tender Heart series. "Was? She's no longer a fan?"

He looked down, his eyes completely expressionless. "My mother died three months ago."

Well, hell. It was hard to stay mad at a man who had just lost his mama.

"Lance hadn't thought it was possible to enjoy fishing with a woman. But not only was Valentine good company . . . she also knew how to bait a hook."

❦

CHAPTER SEVEN

MASON SIPPED HIS MORNING COFFEE and stared at the urn on the windowsill. It was expensive and tasteful just like his mom, which made sense given since she had picked it out. She'd planned her entire funeral long before the cancer had spread through her body. All Mason had to do was show up in Houston and half listen as a never-ending line of his stepfathers stepped up to the pulpit and talked about the woman they'd all loved. It was sad that their love had never been reciprocated.

Men had been disposable to Victoria Granger. If one husband didn't work out, it was easy to get rid of him and find another. As a child, Mason had found this behavior terrifying. He had worked hard to make sure his mother never got tired of him. He catered to her every whim, praised her beauty, and entertained her with stories and jokes.

In college, he reenacted the same needy behavior with the women he dated. But he soon learned that being needy didn't keep women from leaving him. In fact, it only hastened the process. After being hurt more than a few times, he had embraced a dominant nature and embarked on a series of no-strings relationships, with the limits and rules negotiated in advance.

The only woman he couldn't remain detached from was his mother. He thought he'd moved on with his life and put his past insecurities behind him. But now that she was gone, he realized that wasn't true. Her death hurt more than he thought possible, and he was struggling to move on. His work no longer satisfied him. Nor did his sexual partners. He felt adrift, like an empty bottle with no shore to wash onto.

When he'd gone to clean out her house, he'd stumbled upon the worn Tender Heart novels she used to read to him. Something about the novels had struck a chord. Maybe because the only time he had ever felt secure in her love was when he'd been cuddled against her while she read. As a kid, he'd believed in the stories of heroes who didn't shirk their responsibilities. Of heroines who were loving and loyal. And in love that lasted longer than the time it took the ink to dry on a marriage certificate.

Maybe that's why he'd come to Bliss. He was looking for Tender Heart. Not just for his mother, but for himself. He needed to know that somewhere there existed people like the characters in the books. People who loved for a lifetime.

An image of Becky popped into his mind, and he didn't know why. Judging by what he'd read in her diary, she certainly wasn't loyal. He shouldn't have lost his temper and played his dominance game with her, but she'd certainly had no business submitting when she was in love with another man. And she had submitted. There was little doubt that he could've taken her right there against the bathroom wall if he'd wanted to. And he had wanted to. Badly. Honey Bee kept him from it. He didn't play with women who were involved in other relationships—even if they had hungry lips that could drive a man insane.

Pushing the thought away, he got up and took his coffee cup to the sink. Once it was rinsed out, he splashed some cold water on his face. It was still hotter than hell in the house. He'd asked the clerk at the grocery store for names of repair shops, but she'd informed him that there weren't any in Bliss. And the one he'd called in Austin couldn't fit him into their schedule for weeks due to the heat wave. He couldn't take weeks of the heat. The days were bearable, but trying to sleep in a sweltering hot room was impossible. He should head back to Austin and the refrigerated air of his apartment, but he wasn't ready to leave yet.

He dried his face with a paper towel, then retrieved the diary from under his pillow and headed out to the front porch. After last night's kisses, he should probably put the diary back in the floor and forget about it. The steamy sex scenes were probably responsible for what happened in Becky's bathroom. There was no other explanation. He didn't lose control with women. That was his number one rule. Yet he'd lost it with Becky. And if she had given him one more "please," he had little doubt that he would've given her what she asked for.

He stepped out on the porch and stumbled over the gray cat. In his attempt to not step on the mangy animal, he dropped the diary. It slid across the porch and bounced down the steps, landing at a pair of scuffed cowboy boots. Mason looked up from the boots into a smiling face.

"Hey, there." The man picked up the diary, then climbed the steps and held out his hand. "Dirk Hadley. I heard you were having trouble with your air conditioning and I thought I'd stop by and see if I could help."

Mason ignored the hand. "Let me guess. Becky sent you. And not to fix my air conditioner, but to make sure it never works again."

Dirk chuckled. "Obviously you know Becky pretty well." He shook his head. "She's quite the pistol, that one."

"Pistol isn't the word I would use," Mason said dryly. "And thanks for the offer, but I think I'll wait for someone who isn't friends with Becky." He held out his hand. "Book?"

Dirk hesitated before he handed back the diary. "Just for the record, Becky didn't send me. My part in her plan was to make sure you got the worst food in Texas when you came into the diner. I can see burning a man's burger, but I can't see letting him die of this heat. And when Susie at the grocery store told me about your broken air conditioner, I figured I'd come out and offer a hand." He took off his hat and ran the back of his hand across his forehead. "Damn, it's hot. You think I could get a glass of water? I hitched a ride with Daryl Freeman to the turnoff, but I walked the rest of the way." He nodded to the cat, who had yet to move. "I bet your pussycat could use some water too."

"He's not mine. He's a stray." Still, he headed inside to get water for both Dirk and the furball. He was in the process of filling a bowl when Dirk walked into the kitchen followed by the cat. "What the hell?" Mason said. "Don't bring that mangy animal in here."

"I didn't bring him. He came on his own."

He thought about booting the cat out. But since it was already there, he set the bowl of water on the floor. The feline immediately started drinking, which made him feel guilty as hell, and he went to the refrigerator to get some deli turkey. When he turned, he found Dirk staring at the urn on the windowsill.

"Close relative?"

"My mom."

Dirk nodded, but didn't take his eyes off the urn. "My mama was buried. I was only eight at the time and cried like a baby when I saw her in her casket. My granny hugged me close and told me that she'd be with me forever. As I got older, I realized she was talking spiritually. But back then, I couldn't figure out how I'd fit that big casket into my small bedroom in granny's house."

Shit. It looked like Mason now had two pathetic strays to deal with. He tossed Furball the turkey before he turned to Dirk. "You want a beer?"

They drank their beers out on the porch. Mason sat in the rocker with Furball sleeping at his feet, and Dirk sat on the steps with his cowboy hat hooked over one knee. They didn't discuss death.

They talked about the drought, Texas baseball, and the best fishing holes around. When their beers were empty, Mason showed Dirk the air conditioner.

The guy was a handyman. It didn't take him long to figure out what the problem was. Or problems.

"The motor and compressor are shot." Dirk grabbed the hose to wash the grease from his hands. "Rather than fix them, you'd be better off buying a new one. You can order one from Austin, but it will take a few weeks. Or I'm pretty sure Sully Tucker has a used one out at his junkyard. I can have him deliver it here tomorrow and I'll come back tomorrow night after I close the diner and help you install it." He flashed a grin. "Unless you still don't trust me."

Mason shrugged. "I guess I'll have to take my chances."

He gave Dirk a ride back into town, and they stopped by the junkyard on the way and made the arrangements with Sully to deliver a used air conditioning unit the following day. Then he dropped Dirk at the diner. Before he got out, Dirk turned to Mason.

"As the baby girl of her family, Becky can be a bit of a brat. But her desire for the Reed place isn't a spoiled child's whim. She wants it more for her cousin Gracie than for herself."

"What does her cousin have to do with it?"

"I guess Becky and Gracie used to dream about ranching the Reed property together. Now that it looks like Gracie won't walk again, Becky wants to make sure she gets her dream."

Mason had heard about Gracie from Zane. A young woman being thrown from her horse and becoming paralyzed was a tragic accident. It was admirable to want to help her. But he had to wonder if Becky wasn't just using her cousin to get her hands on his ranch.

"The house isn't exactly set up for someone in a wheelchair," he said.

"If Gracie wants to live there, I'd be willing to do the work to make sure she can get around it. Of course, that's neither here nor there, since you own the house and the ranch it sits on." He tapped the bottom edge of the open window. "Thanks for the ride, Mace."

After leaving Dirk at the diner, Mason headed back to the house. But it was too damned hot to stay inside. So he loaded up a cooler with beer, left Furball snoozing on the porch, and headed to one of the fishing holes Dirk had told him about. He didn't realize that the fishing hole was on Zane and Becky's land until he was waved over by a guy in a truck with Earhart Ranch stenciled on the side.

Once the man rolled down his window, Mason recognized him as the ranch hand who had come out to help when they brought back the wounded calf. The man seemed almost hostile until he recognized Mason.

"You're Becky's friend that helped with the calf." Mason wouldn't go as far as to call them friends, but he nodded. The man reached a hand out the window. "I'm Jess Owens, the foreman of the Earhart Ranch."

Mason took his hand and gave it a firm shake.

"Mason Granger. How is the calf doing?"

"Good. Although we had to call out the vet and have him stitch up the deeper cuts that weren't caused by the barbed wire."

Mason was confused. "What were they caused by?"

Jess pushed up his hat and used a bandana to wipe the sweat off his face. "The vet seems to think that they were knife wounds. And after taking a closer look, I have to agree. Barbed wire pokes and tears the skin in a jagged line. But these cuts were clean and straight. And it was weird how they formed a perfect X over the Earhart brand."

That was weird. Too weird to be a coincidence. He had to wonder if Ms. Marble's concerns about Becky's stalker were entirely unfounded.

"Where's Becky?" he asked.

"That's who I was looking for when I ran into you. After seeing those cuts, I told her to stay close to the house. But that girl has never listened well. Especially now that Zane's gone. She's been running herself ragged trying to prove she can handle the ranch on her own."

Mason shouldn't get involved. Becky wasn't his concern. But with Zane out of town, he couldn't help feeling responsible. "Where have you looked? If we split the rest of the ranch up between us, we'll find her quicker."

It still took a good hour to find Becky's truck. It was parked by a cluster of trees not too far from the ranch house. He called Jess to let him know, then headed along the path that lead through the trees. When he stepped into the clearing, he froze in stunned awe.

He'd visited some of the most beautiful cathe-
drals in the world during his travels, but not one
had made him feel as emotional as the little white
chapel did. It looked exactly like it had been
described in the Tender Heart books. Its white
siding contrasted sharply with the vibrant green
trees that surrounded it and the deep-blue sky. On
the sides of the church were three multi-colored
stained-glass windows, each depicting a different
Texas flower. A tall spire stretched up to the heav-
ens, its metal bell reflecting the hot afternoon sun
like a godly wink.

Mason stood there for a moment absorbing the
beauty of the church before he walked down the
cobblestone path to the sturdy oak doors. Once
inside, he was surprised by how cool it felt . . . and
reverently holy. He took off his cowboy hat and
looked around for Becky. He checked the back
rooms, then made his way to the altar. He found
her stretched out in the third pew with her boots
crossed and her head resting on a bible. Her cowboy hat covered her face, and he could hear her
snores through the holes in the straw.

He shook his head, but couldn't help the smile
that tipped his lips. The woman had a style all
her own. He thought about tapping her boot to
wake her up. But then he remembered what Jess
had said and decided to let her sleep. Dirk had
also mentioned that Becky wanted to prove herself to her father and Zane. Mason had never met
her father, but he did know Zane. He got along
with his friend, but he recognized a control freak
when he saw one. He didn't doubt for a second
that Zane ran the ranch his way and wouldn't put

too much value on his sister's opinions. Especially when she was such a hothead.

A hothead who might have a dangerous stalker.

"Something had changed between her and Lance, and Valentine didn't know if that was a good thing or a bad thing."

C

CHAPTER EIGHT

BECKY WAS HAVING A WEIRD dream. She was lying in a field of flowers completely naked and covered in bees. Honeybees. Except she didn't feel like she was covered in bees. They weren't stinging her or crawling on her with their tiny, creepy legs. Instead, she felt like she was cocooned inside a snuggly blanket. The bees held her tightly, but they weren't restrictive. She knew that if she really wanted to move, the bees would let her. But for now, she didn't want to move. She felt secure and content, almost like she was the queen of the hive and every bee was there to serve her.

She sighed. "Honeybees."

A scornful snort disrupted the bees, and they scattered to the wind, leaving Becky blinking awake and stare at the tiny holes in her straw cowboy hat. She removed the hat and smiled at the sturdy beams that formed a peak in the ceiling.

The little white chapel.

"I guess you know you snore."

The feeling of contentment vanished, and she

sat straight up to find Mason slouched at the end of the pew with an open bible in his hands. His cowboy hat was hooked on the corner of the pew in front and his dark hair was mussed and sexy. Yes, sexy. After a sleepless night, she'd come to terms with the fact that she was sexually attracted to Mason. She had never begged a man in her life, and yet she would've gotten down on her hands and knees for one more kiss from Mason. Which was disturbing. Extremely disturbing.

"What are you doing here—" She stopped when she realized what he'd said. "I do not snore."

He cocked one eyebrow. "Hasn't your boyfriend mentioned it?"

"Not that it's any of your business, but I don't have a boyfriend. And even if I did, he wouldn't be rude enough to mention my snoring—not that I snore."

He studied her as if he was trying to figure out if she was lying, and she had to wonder why he was so interested in her dating status when it was obvious that he didn't like her. Of course, you didn't have to like someone to want them. She'd figured that out as soon as Mason had touched her. If his kisses were any indication, he wouldn't be a gentle lover. Sex with Mason would be one wild ride. And Becky had always liked her rides wild.

She pushed the thought away. She couldn't have sex with Mason. He was the only thing standing between her and the Reed ranch. She couldn't let a little desire—or a lot—get in the way of her and Gracie's dream.

"So what are you doing here?" She glanced at

the bible. "Besides repenting for all your sins."

A smile played at the corners of his mouth, but didn't win out over his usual somber expression. He closed the bible and slid it into the holder on the back of the pew. "I'm afraid I'm not much on repenting. I ran into Jess, and he was worried about you after what happened to the calf." He turned to her, his eyes intense. "Tell me about Rich."

The question shocked her. "Who told you about Rich?"

"It doesn't matter who told me. I want you to tell me about him. Or more specifically about how he's been stalking you."

She laughed and got to her feet. "He's not stalking me. He just likes me." She headed out of the pew.

He came the opposite way and arrived at the door before she did, blocking her exit. "And do you like him?"

"No. He's a little too aggressive for my tastes."

His eyebrows lifted. "Too aggressive?"

She wasn't a blusher, but the question had her cheeks flushing with heat. Mason had been aggressive. More than aggressive. And she hadn't minded in the least. In fact, she'd begged for more.

"I mean he wouldn't stop when I told him no."

Mason's surprised look turned to dark anger. "Did he hurt you?"

"No. The only one who got hurt was Rich when I kneed him where it counts. Unfortunately, he didn't take the hint and he kept sending me flowers and leaving gifts in my truck. Since I stomped the teddy bear, I think he's finally gotten the message that I'm not interested." She skirted around him and pushed open the door. The humid heat was like being dunked in a scalding tub of water, and she wasted no time heading to her truck and its air conditioner. Mason's long strides easily caught up with her.

"That could be why Rich retaliated by slicing up one of your cows. He's sending you a message. And that message is don't stomp on my gifts."

She stopped and turned to him. "Jess told you about the cuts?" She needed to have a talk with her foreman about gossiping about ranch business.

"He's worried about you. And so is Ms. Marble. She thinks Rich is stalking you, and I'm starting to agree with her. Especially after the calf."

"Rich didn't do that. It was probably some delinquent high school kid. They get antsy in the summer and look for things to do. They steal cows and leave them on their girlfriends' front lawns with bovine love poems. They spray paint *Eat Mor Chikin* on their butts. Yes, this was a little more cruel than normal. But I don't think it's anything to freak out about." She paused. "Why *are* you so freaked out?"

"Because you're Zane's little sister, and he'd do the same for me if I had a little sister who needed a keeper. Now where does this guy live so I can talk to him?"

The little sister thing annoyed her. "You don't need to protect me, Mason. I'm a big girl. A big girl who needs to get back to work." She turned to leave, but he grabbed her arm and pulled her against him. Her breath rushed out in a whoosh when she met the hard planes of his body. His hands tightened on her waist, and yet, she didn't feel like he held her prisoner. She felt as content as she had with the bees in her dream.

"This isn't one of your cowboys that you can intimidate with your family name and aggressive nature," he said. "If this guy is the one responsible for the calf, then he doesn't mind drawing blood. And the next time, he could take out his displeasure on you. Do you understand?"

The only thing she understood was that after months of looking for the all-consuming fire that Lucy had written about in her diary, here it was. Burning her insides with its heat and making her forget about dreams and ranches.

"Answer me, Rebecca."

The deep, sexy way he said her name caused the last of her resistance to melt away. She couldn't fight the desire anymore. She didn't want to fight it. She stared into his beautiful brown eyes and whispered the one word she'd sworn she would never speak to him again. "Please."

His eyes registered shock before they turned to sizzling coals. He growled low in his throat before he lowered his head and kissed her. This time, he wasn't as rough. This time, his lips softly plucked before he deepened the kiss and caressed the inside of her mouth with his tongue. Her knees turned to water, and she clung to him like a raft in turbulent rapids. She had spent her entire life trying to prove she didn't need a man for anything. But Mason changed that. She needed him. She needed him to quench the fire he'd started, and she was thoroughly disappointed when he drew back from the kiss and released her.

"I think we need to get something straight."

It was annoying that he didn't look even slightly fazed by the hot kiss, while she was struggling to keep from melting at his feet. She locked her knees and crossed her arms to hide her trembling hands. "What do you want to get straight this time? If it's about Rich, I don't want to hear it. I made the mistake of dating him. I'll be the one to handle him."

He released his breath in an exasperated sigh. "Fine. But if you won't let me talk to him, at least let me give you some advice as a lawyer. You need to keep a record of everything that has happened since you broke it off with him. How many times he's texted and called you. How many times he's shown up at places where you were. And how many times he's gotten into your truck without your permission and left something. If you have to file a restraining order, you'll want to have that information."

She didn't think she'd need a restraining order, but maybe she should keep track of Rich's harassment just in case. "Thanks for the advice. Now if you're finished getting things straight, I need to get back to work."

He stepped in front of her. "Rich wasn't what I wanted to get straight." His expression turned softer, almost sympathetic. "I can't be your lover, Rebecca."

Even though that's exactly what she'd been thinking, she bristled at his arrogance. "And who said I wanted you as a lover, Granger?"

A hint of a smile tipped his mouth. "I know desire when I see it. You desire me. And it's pretty obvious that I desire you." The fact that he desired her made her a lot less annoyed. "But no matter how much I desire you, I'm not going to take you to bed. Not only because you're Zane's sister, but because you're the type of woman who wants roses and romance." He glanced at the church. "And eventually, a wedding in a little white chapel. But I don't do weddings. I don't even do girlfriends." He paused for only a second before he continued. "I'm a dominant. Do you know what that means?"

It took her a moment to process the word. When her brain finally did, she couldn't help staring at him in shock. "Are we talking Christian Grey?"

He visibly cringed. "Yes, but not quite as disturbed. I don't have a red room with whips and chains. I'm not into extreme pain. I just like my women to follow my commands without expecting anything but pleasure in return."

Becky didn't know why she suddenly felt a little lightheaded. Maybe because she'd had a taste of the pleasure Mason offered and her body craved more. She swallowed hard. "So you don't want a long commitment? You just want to give pleasure?"

He gave one brief nod. With that nod, Becky made her decision.

Mason Granger was going to be her Honey Bee.

> *"Lance didn't know why the cowboy's comment ticked him off. Valentine was asking for it, strutting around town in the indecent, low-cut dress. Regardless, only a few seconds after the bosom comment, Lance was standing over the knocked-out cowboy massaging his sore knuckles, while Valentine stared at him like he'd sprouted horns."*

&

CHAPTER NINE

BEING A LAWYER HAD ITS perks. When you needed information about someone, you had plenty of resources. Mason had Rich Myer's address by the following morning. Rich lived a good twenty minutes outside of Bliss on a rural road that Mason drove past and had to backtrack to find. His trailer was set amid some overgrown pecan trees. The siding was rusted, two of the windows were broken out, and the front door looked like a wild animal had mauled it. The door was so beat up that Mason had to search for a solid place to knock.

Not that he expected an answer. There were no vehicles parked in front—at least not with any tires. Mason was more than a little disappointed. He'd looked forward to putting the fear of God in the man. Becky was convinced Rich hadn't been the one who cut the calf, and maybe she was right. But the guy was still harassing her and needed to stop.

When no one answered his knock, he leaned over from the dilapidated front steps and looked in the window. The place was a pigsty. Beer cans, pizza boxes, and filled ashtrays covered the kitchen table. But it wasn't the mess that caught his attention as much as the collage of pictures on the wall leading into the living room.

Every single one was of Becky.

He didn't even try the door to see if it was locked. He just lifted a boot and kicked it in. It rebounded off the wall with a loud bang. If Rich was at home, Mason had just been announced.

The place stunk like smoke, beer, and body odor. He walked straight over to the pictures that had been carefully taped to the wall. Becky hadn't posed for any of them. She looked completely unaware that someone was photographing her. That pissed him off. He became even more pissed when he saw the one of her skinny-dipping. It was from far enough away that you couldn't see details, but close enough to know she was naked.

"Sonofabitch!" He started to jerk the picture off the wall, but then stopped. The pictures were evidence that Rich was stalking Becky. They needed to stay right here until she could be convinced to press charges and push for a search warrant. There was little doubt that somewhere in the trailer or in the guy's vehicle was the knife that had been used to cut the calf.

He left, not bothering to close the door behind him. He hoped the busted door scared Rich. He hoped it scared him enough to get the hell out of Texas, but he doubted it. Stalkers were obsessed with their prey. Nothing short of jail time would stop their infatuation. And sometimes not even that. Which meant that until Rich was locked up, Becky was in danger.

Mason just wished he could get that through her head. If he couldn't, maybe her brother could. As soon as he was on the highway, he called Zane.

"Mace?" Zane answered in a groggy voice.

"Sorry, man." Mason glanced at the dash clock. "I forgot about the time difference."

"No problem." Zane yawned. "Carly and I need to rise and shine anyway. She signed us up for some snorkeling excursion today—even though I told the woman that cowboys aren't exactly waterproof."

Mason heard Carly's laughter in the background. "You were last night in the hot tub."

"That's because I was diving for pearls."

There was giggling as if Zane was tickling Carly, and just that quickly, Mason realized his mistake. He'd thought he would be helping his friend by watching out for his little sister. Instead, he'd be ruining his honeymoon. Zane was extremely protective of Becky. Once he heard about Rich, he'd want to hop the first flight home. And Mason couldn't let him do that. Not when there was another way to protect Becky.

"So what's up?" Zane asked.

"I was just calling to see if it would be okay if I stayed at your ranch for a few days. My air conditioner is broken and the heat here has been pretty unbearable."

Zane didn't hesitate. "Of course you can stay at the house. In fact, it will put my mind at ease knowing someone is there to keep an eye on Becky. With my dad in Houston at a livestock show, I'm a little worried about her being in charge."

As far as Mason could tell, Becky didn't have problem being in charge. She had a problem listening to reason. He would have his hands full trying to convince her to file charges against Rich.

"And could I ask another favor?" Zane continued. "Do you think you could get Becky away from the ranch next Friday? It's her birthday and my mother is cooking up a little birthday surprise for her. My daddy should be there by then, but getting Becky to spend the entire day with Daddy is asking a lot."

"I thought you were going to be gone for two weeks."

"That's all part of the plan to throw Becky off. She always expects a surprise party. So this year we planned it for the day before her actual birthday. I hope you can be there. I had my mom send the invitation to your apartment in Austin. I didn't realize you were going to be in Bliss this soon. Are you getting in some rest and relaxation?"

The last few days had been anything but relaxing, so Mason needed to stretch the truth. "I've done a little reading and a little sightseeing, and I plan to do some fishing. And speaking of fishing, I better let you get to your snorkeling. Enjoy the rest of your honeymoon. I'll see you when you get back."

"See you then. And tell my baby sister to behave herself—not that she'll listen."

"Will do," Mason said before he hung up. Although he didn't need to remind Becky as much as himself. The kiss he'd given her at the little white chapel had almost sent him over the edge. He'd been seconds away from taking her right then and there. The only thing that had kept him from it was the fact that they didn't play by the same rules, which was why he made a point of letting her know about his sexual preferences. Now that she knew, he had little doubt that she would stay completely away from him. She wanted sweet, gentle lovers like Honey Bee. Although Honey Bee was no longer her lover.

After she said she didn't have a boyfriend, he'd been curious. He'd left the chapel and gone straight back to his house to finish reading the diary. Becky hadn't lied. The last entry was only two short lines.

Honey Bee is gone. My heart is broken forever.

It was a little dramatic. Especially when Becky didn't act heartbroken. She acted like she was ready for another lover. Just not Mason.

When he got back to his house, he found Ms. Marble's Oldsmobile parked out front. Since he couldn't see her sitting in the car and he was pretty sure he'd locked the front door, he worried that she'd passed out in the front seat from the heat. But she wasn't in the car. He searched around the house, and then hurried up the porch steps. He'd been wrong. The front door was unlocked.

Once inside, he noticed three things: The cool air. The delicious scent wafting from the kitchen.

And the mangy cat curled up right in the center of the rug in the living room. It opened one green eye and stared at him for a moment before closing it and going back to sleep.

Mason walked into the kitchen where he found the little old woman puttering around like the last time she'd been there. And like before, the sight made him feel strangely content.

"Well, there you are," she said when she saw him. She walked over and leaned up to give him a kiss on the cheek. "I thought you'd gone back to Austin and left me on my own. I hope you don't mind me making myself at home. I was afraid if I left my oatmeal chocolate chip cookies on the porch, the chocolate would be nothing but a gooey mess by the time you got back."

She moved to the table and unwrapped the plate of cookies. "I knew you loved chocolate by the way you gobbled up my brownies, but the oatmeal will keep you regular." She sent him a stern look. "I'm convinced that's one of the reasons you never smile. Constipation is not a laughing matter."

Mason laughed. The woman was a character. "Thank you for caring about my digestive system."

"Everyone needs someone to care about them. And seeing as how you don't have any family to watch out for you, it falls to your friends." She poured some sweet tea into the glasses on the table. "Speaking of which, I'm glad to see you've made friends with Dirk. When I got here, I found him inside testing the air conditioner."

Obviously, the people of Bliss didn't have a

problem walking into houses uninvited. "It feels like it works pretty good."

She smiled. "That boy is handy. Now come sit down and have some tea." She pulled a stack of legal-sized paper out of the tote bag hooked on the back of the kitchen chair. "And while we're at it, you can look over my will before I keel over."

Mason took off his cowboy hat and tossed it onto the counter before taking the chair next to hers. "I think you've got a few good years left in you."

Her blue eyes twinkled. "Maybe just a few."

After he finished going over Ms. Marble's will and correcting any problems he saw, he walked her to the door. She smiled at the cat that was now stretched out on the rug like a fur blanket with paws. She squeezed his arm. "Only a sensitive man with a heart of gold can understand a feline."

Mason didn't have a heart of gold. Once Ms. Marble was gone, he turned to the cat. "Enjoy your nap, Furball. When I finish lunch, you're out on your ass."

But while he was eating, Furball came into the kitchen and sat by his feet. It was hard to ignore the pleading look in the green eyes. He ended up giving the cat half the ham from his sandwich. When he went to the bedroom to pack, Furball followed him and jumped up on the bed.

"Oh no, you don't." Mason grabbed the cat and then wrinkled his nose. "Damn, you smell worse than Rich Myer's trailer." He should've tossed the stinky thing outside. Instead, he carried the cat to the bathroom.

He learned a couple things about cats while giving Furball a bath: Cats don't like water. And they have extremely sharp claws. By the time the stink was off the mangy animal, Mason had numerous scratches on his arms. As soon as he toweled the cat off and set it on the floor, Furball streaked under the bed and stayed there while Mason finished packing.

He packed light. He didn't plan on staying at the Earhart Ranch during the day. He figured Rich wasn't brave enough to bother Becky with a bunch of ranch hands around. And maybe he wasn't brave enough to bother her at all. Maybe he was the type of guy who was only brave with helpless animals. But Mason wasn't willing to take the chance.

He was almost finished packing when he dropped a balled-up pair of boot socks on the floor. The cat finally came out from under the bed to attack the rolling socks. It was hard not to laugh at the pouncing and batting that ensued. The ball of socks ended up in the corner. Furball pounced on them and the loose board popped up and smacked him in the butt, causing the cat to yowl and streak from the room.

Mason was still laughing when he walked over to retrieve his socks. The loose board reminded him that he needed to put the diary back in the floor. Or maybe he should just give it to Becky. He tossed his socks in the suitcase, then reached under the pillow.

The diary was gone.

"Valentine Clemens had spent her entire life fighting for herself. A champion was not something she was used to. Especially one who made her heart flutter and her knees weak with just one look from his dark, penetrating eyes."

☙

CHAPTER TEN

"YOU WANT MASON AS YOUR Honey Bee?" Gracie's yelled so loudly that Becky had to pull the phone away from her ear. "Are you crazy? You can't have some guy you hate as your Honey Bee."

"I never said I hated him." Becky opened the door of the stall. As soon as she stepped inside, Muffin came over to greet her. The foal immediately started nosing Becky's pockets for the treats she always brought him. She pulled out a carrot stub and gave it to the horse. "I just said he was too controlling."

"But I thought you hated controlling men?"

She did. But she'd come to realize that Mason wasn't controlling as much as . . . *dominant.*

Just the word sent a tingle of heat to Becky's panties. She'd read the *Fifty Shades* book her senior year in college because all her friends were reading it. And while she didn't love it nearly as much as the Tender Heart series, it had conjured up a lot of fantasies. Fantasies that had been resurrected after Mason had told her about his kink. She spent another sleepless night wondering just how kinky he got. Did he use ropes? Cuffs? A riding crop?

"Becky?"

Becky blinked away the fantasy and returned to the conversation. "I realize you want your Honey Bee to be a man you love, Gracie Lynn. But I'm not ready for love. Starting a ranch is a full-time job and I don't need to add a husband to the mix—or even a serious boyfriend. Which is why Mason is so perfect. He doesn't want a serious relationship either. Besides, if I have sex with him it could work in our favor."

"How do you figure?"

"There's nothing like a clingy woman to make a man head for the hills."

There was a long pause before Gracie spoke. "I still don't think it's a good idea. Can't you just offer him more money when you get your trust fund?"

"I could, but I get the feeling that money doesn't mean that much to Mason."

"Actually, money means quite a lot to me."

Becky whirled around to see Mason leaning on the lower half of the stable door. His dark eyes twinkled with amusement. She had never seen Mason amused before. It made him even more devilishly handsome. It also made her wonder how much he'd overheard.

"I have to call you later, Gracie," she said before she hung up the phone and slipped it into the back pocket of her jeans. "Do you always slip around listening in on peoples' conversations?"

"Only when they're talking about me. Who were you talking to?"

"My cousin."

A calculating look entered his eyes. "Ahh, since disrupting my peace and quiet hasn't worked, you're going to try bribery."

She smiled and shrugged. "I figured it couldn't hurt."

He didn't seem angry. Only amused. "You're certainly tenacious. I'll give you that."

"My daddy calls it stubbornness."

"Is your cousin as stubborn?"

"When she wants something, she can be. But she's not as vocal about it as I am." She gave Muffin another carrot stub before she headed for the door. Mason stepped back as she opened it. The cat sitting at his feet took her by surprise. "Just where did you come from, sweetheart?" She knelt down and scratched the cat's ears.

"The bowels of hell, I think," Mason said.

"Don't listen to him. He's just a Mr. Grumpy Pants." She got to her feet and sent him a quizzical look. "You're a cat guy?"

Beneath the brim of his cowboy hat, his eyebrows lowered. "No. I'm not a cat guy. Furball just showed up at my house. I even considered the possibility that you sent him to torment me."

"I have a lot of abilities, but cat mind control isn't one of them." She headed over to the shelves where they kept the cat and dog foods. She filled a bowl and placed it on the ground. The cat remained by Mason's boots and lifted his nose in disdain. She looked at Mason. "You've been feeding him people food, haven't you?"

The blush that stained his cheeks made her laugh, and his scowl deepened. "What the hell was I supposed to do? Let him starve? I brought him here because I thought you might need a mouser—"

Shep came racing in the door of the barn after spending his day herding cattle in the fields. The dog liked cats, but Mason didn't know that. He scooped the cat up and cradled it protectively against his chest as Shep jumped around his legs.

Becky laughed. "Admit it, Mason, you're now the owner of a cute kitty."

His eyes narrowed. "I am not—" His shoulders slumped. "Fine. I'm a cat guy." He looked so distraught that she couldn't continue to tease him.

"Go ahead and put him down," she said. "Shep loves cats."

He hesitated for only a second before he placed the cat on the ground. Shep came over with his tail wagging. The cat wasn't as friendly. It arched and hissed. When Shep backed up, the cat jumped on a hay bale and watched the dog from a higher perch.

Mason visibly relaxed. "Good. The mangy thing can stay out in the barn while I'm here?"

"While you're here?"

He crossed his arms and stared her down. "I'm staying in the guestroom until Zane gets back. Or until you press charges against Rich."

His stance said he was prepared for a fight, but Becky was through fighting Mason. She was ready to surrender to the chemistry between them and make him her Honey Bee. It looked like fate was on her side. She thought she'd have to go to the Reed ranch to seduce him, but he had come to her.

"Just what are you smiling about?" he asked. "Being stalked is not a laughing matter."

"You're right. I guess I'm still thinking about you being a cat guy." She turned so he wouldn't see her smile get any bigger. "Come on. I'll show you the guestroom."

Once she'd shown Mason to his room, she headed to hers for a long, hot shower. It had been a hard day on the ranch and she couldn't seduce a man smelling like road kill. She couldn't help wishing that Mason would bust in like he had before, and she was thoroughly disappointed when he didn't.

After her shower, she blow-dried her hair and put on the scented lotion Gracie had given her for Christmas. She wanted to put on something sexy and feminine, but her wardrobe was dismally lacking in that department. So she chose a pair of Daisy Duke jean shorts and a white t-shirt. Then she fluffed her hair, put on a dab of lip gloss, and went to find her houseguest. She found him in the kitchen standing over the stove stirring something that smelled delicious. Again, she was surprised.

"A cat guy and a cook?"

He turned, his gaze taking in her hair before lowering to her white t-shirt. Since she hadn't put on a bra, there was little doubt he could see her nipples through the thin cotton. She was play-ing with fire, but she didn't care. She was almost twenty-five and ready to get burned. She straight-ened her shoulders and tried to subtly thrust her chest out so her boobs looked bigger and more tempting.

He wasn't tempted. He turned back to the stove and continued their conversation. "I assume you don't cook."

"Only when forced." She stared at his dark, wavy hair that fell on the back of his neck. She really wanted to run her fingers through those inky locks, then tug him around so she could hungrily feast on his sweet lips. But that would be too aggressive. And Mason didn't want aggressive. He wanted submissive. But how could she be submissive and still get the point across that she wanted to make him her Honey Bee? Maybe she just needed to come out and say it. But before she could, he plated up the chicken and vegetable stir-fry. The delicious-looking food, coupled with the fact that she hadn't eaten all day, made her postpone her declaration. There would be plenty of time to talk after dinner.

Once they were seated at the breakfast bar, he expertly uncorked the Chardonnay he must've brought and poured it in a glass before handing it to her. "Or would you rather have milk?"

She ignored the dig at her age and accepted the glass. "I'd rather have a beer, but wine is fine." Although she didn't even take a sip before she dug into her food. It was delicious. "So where did you learn to cook?" she asked in between bites.

"My mom liked to cook. I learned by watching her."

"Were you close to your mother?"

He took a deep drink of his wine. "No male ever got close to my mother. She didn't allow it."

The statement was spoken with no emotion, and yet every word was filled with pain. Becky's mother wasn't exactly warm and fuzzy, but she never failed to show her kids how much she loved them. Becky had to wonder about a woman who wouldn't let her son get close. After that conversation killer, they ate in silence. It wasn't until they were almost finished that Mason spoke again. The man could fixate on things.

"Are you going to call the sheriff about Rich or not?"

"Not."

He released an exasperated sigh. "I didn't want to scare you. But since you're being so stubborn, you need to know that I went to his trailer and he has a wall of pictures of you."

She set down her fork. "You went to Rich's trailer? How did you know where he lives?"

"Lawyers have connections. Now are you going to call the sheriff?"

"And tell him what? That Rich keeps leaving me love notes and teddy bears? Or that you saw pictures of me at his trailer? Last I heard, it wasn't a crime to take pictures of people."

"Even when they're skinny dipping?"

She cringed. "Okay, that's creepy."

"Exactly. So are you going to call the sheriff? Hopefully, next time he can catch Rich in the act of stalking you."

"There won't be a next time." She got up and carried her plate to the sink.

"What do you mean there won't be a next time?" He got up and moved around the breakfast bar.

"I mean that Rich texted me today and I texted him back and told him to leave me the hell alone."

"Didn't you try that before and the guy still didn't get the hint?"

"Yes, but this time I told him I have another boyfriend." She glanced over to see his brow knitted.

"I thought you said you didn't have a boyfriend. Who is it?"

She rinsed off her plate before she turned to him and smiled. "You. I've decided to submit."

"Lance should've been relieved that Etta Jenkins was now bringing all the women's complaints. And yet, he wasn't relieved. He missed Valentine."

℺

CHAPTER ELEVEN

BY THE TIME MASON GOT over his shock, Becky was bent over the dishwasher putting away her plate. He took her arm and whirled her around. "You are not going to be my submissive."

Her eyes twinkled with mischief before she quickly lowered them. "Yes, sir."

"Stop that!"

She kept her head bowed. "Stop what, sir?"

He gave her a little shake. "I mean it, Rebecca. This isn't funny anymore. You can't just decide to be a submissive. That's not how it works."

She lifted her head and looked thoroughly confused. "Why not? Don't tell me there are submissive classes? I mean how hard can it be? You tell me what to do and I listen."

"Wrong. It's not just about bossing someone around in the bedroom. A submissive has just as much control as the dominant—more so. They are the ones who set the limitations. The ones who stop play when those limitations are in danger of being broken."

She waved a hand as if to dismiss what he'd just said. "I already know all about limits and safe words. I think we should use colors because they're self-explanatory. Green means go. Yellow means 'Slow down, I'm not too sure I like this.' And red means 'Stop! That hurts!'" She sent him a satisfied smile like a student who'd gotten the answer right. And the fact that she'd put so much time and thought into being his submissive made Mason a little speechless . . . and a lot horny.

"See," she continued, "I've got this."

He shook his head. Not only to get it across that she didn't have it, but also to clear any crazy thoughts—like making Becky his submissive. "No. You don't have it. I'm not making you my submissive."

"Why not? Is this about Zane? I promise you don't have to worry about me running to my big brother and tattling. That's not my style." Her gaze lowered to the open neck of his snap-down western shirt. "Besides, who I take as a lover is nobody's business." She reached out and pressed her finger to the indentation at the base of his throat. Just one little finger, and his cock turned as hard as the granite counter top behind her. "I desire you," she whispered as she slid that hot digit down to the first closed snap and back up again. "And you said you desired me." Her gaze lifted to reveal the hot simmering blue of her eyes. "So why shouldn't we have a little fun?"

A little fun? Obviously, she didn't have a clue what she was asking for. She didn't understand that being a submissive could involve a darker pleasure that included more pain than just a playful smack on the bottom. And maybe the only way to make her understand was to give her a taste of how rough things could get.

He fisted his hand in her hair and tugged her head back. Her blue eyes flashed with surprise, which only confirmed that she didn't know what she was asking for.

"Fine," he growled. "You want a little fun? I'll give you a little fun." He scooped her up in his arms and carried her to her bedroom. He tossed her unceremoniously onto the mattress and jerked open the snaps of his shirt. "Get naked."

She scooted back against the headboard. "Umm . . . shouldn't we talk a little first. Maybe get the limitations ironed out."

"Why would we mess with that when you know your safe words?" He unhooked his belt and jerked it from the loops with a snap of leather against denim.

She jumped. "Okay, but if I don't like it, I can stop it whenever I want. The submissive really has all the control. Right?"

He moved toward the bed. "That's true, but I have a little problem with self-control. Once I get into it, I have trouble stopping."

She visibly swallowed. "Oh."

He doubled the belt and snapped it with a loud cracking sound that made her jump again. "So what's it going to be, Rebecca? You want me as your lover?"

Time ticked by as he waited for her to make her decision. From the look of her wide blue eyes, he thought he knew what it was going to be. Which was why his jaw dropped when she stripped off her shirt. Obviously, Becky wasn't one who backed down after she made up her mind. He barely got over the view of her sweet rosy-tipped breasts when she pushed down her shorts. He'd gotten a glimpse of her body when she stepped from the shower, but now he got to look his fill as she climbed off the high mattress and stood before him in all her naked glory.

"Just remember I bruise easily." She turned and bent over the bed.

Mason's knees went weak at the sight of those full, pale cheeks and long, toned legs. He swallowed hard and tried to get a grip on the desire that pooled hot and heavy in his loins. But when he lifted the belt, his hand shook so badly he had to lower it and take a deep breath.

All he needed to do was give her one good swat. Just enough to show her that this wasn't a game she wanted to play. Just one good swat, and she'd be begging for him to stop. He gritted his teeth and lifted the belt, bringing it down with just enough force to make a smacking sound against the fullest part of her ass. She flinched, and he waited for her to scream stop. Instead, there was a long silence.

A red mark sprung up on her perfect cheeks, and damned if Mason wasn't the one who wanted to yell stop. He was about to when Becky finally spoke.

"Is that it?"

Mason blinked. "Excuse me?"

Becky glanced over her shoulder. Her hair curved over one eye and down her back in waves of golden brown. "I just thought that sex with you would be a little rougher."

"Rougher?" He dropped the belt. "You want rougher?" He smacked her ass with his open hand. "Is that what you had in mind, Rebecca?" When she didn't reply, he smacked her again and again until her butt was bright red.

He rolled her onto her back, expecting to see tears or anger. Instead, he saw desire. Hot, unmistakable desire that shimmered in her blue eyes and melted any logical thinking he was still trying to hold onto. When she ran her fingers through his hair and pulled him down to her waiting lips, he was the one to submit.

He submitted to the heat of her mouth and the sweetness of her tongue. To the gentleness of her fingers and softness of her body. He submitted to the light that was Becky. A light that seemed to search out and penetrate the darkness inside of him, flooding it and consuming it until it no longer existed. For once, he didn't feel lost. He felt found. And he didn't want the feeling to end. He never wanted it to end. In fact, he wanted to go deeper into the light.

Without breaking the kiss, he rolled to the side and undid the button and zipper of his jeans. He had his boots on, but he didn't want to leave her long enough to pull them off. So he merely shoved down his jeans before reaching for his wallet where he kept a condom. Once it was on, he adjusted her leg over his hips and thrust deep.

She broke the kiss and yelled. "Red!"

He froze. Not only at the word, but also the tight barrier he broke through to heavenly heat.

Becky might've dated a lot of guys, but she hadn't had sex with them. Not even Honey Bee.

"You're a virgin?" His voice was hoarse and strained from trying not to move.

"Not anymore." At the smartass remark, he started to pull out, but she tightened her leg around him. And she had strong legs. "Oh no, you don't. Now that the worst part is over, I'm ready for the good stuff." She thrust her hips and took him deeper. For a second, he thought he was going to come right then and there.

He spoke through his teeth. "Don't move."

"Sorry, but you had your chance to be dominant. Now it's my turn." She pushed him onto his back and followed, straddling him and sheathing him in her tight heat. His body begged him to thrust. Instead, he remained perfectly still. Unfortunately, Becky didn't. Her hips started moving and any gentlemanly thought of stopping completely disappeared.

She wasn't experienced at sex, but she figured it out quickly enough. After a few awkward bounces, she found a smooth rocking motion that made him grind his head back into the mattress. She must've liked it too because she moaned. And the more she rocked and moaned, the more Mason struggled to hold on. When she finally tipped back her head and released a throaty groan as she reached orgasm, he lost it.

He grabbed her hips and thrust until he was spent. Then he flopped back on the bed and flung an arm over his eyes. "Shit."

Becky melted against his chest. "I'd like to second that. Holy shit."

He opened his eyes and stared up at the ceiling. "I didn't mean it in a good way."

She lifted her head. "You didn't like it?"

He had liked it. He'd liked it too damned much. But that wasn't the problem. "Why didn't you tell me you were a virgin?"

The hurt in her eyes cleared, and she moved off of him. Although she didn't go far. She cuddled up to his side like she belonged there. "Oh, that's what has you so grumpy."

"I'm not grumpy." He placed his hands behind his head so he wouldn't be tempted to pull her closer. "I'm pissed that you didn't tell me you were a virgin."

"You didn't ask."

It ticked him off that she would try to put the blame on him. "Why would I ask? You're almost twenty-five, for God sake, and wrote about screwing Honey Bee in your diary!"

She lifted her head, her eyes wide. "You found Lucy's diary and thought it was mine?" When all he could do was stare at her in confusion, she rolled onto her back and starting laughing.

He sat up, now more annoyed than ever. "And just who is Lucy—" He stopped. "Lucy Arrington?"

She grinned. "That would be the one. Didn't you see her name on the inside cover?"

"I saw Rebecca Lucille Arrington on the inside cover. I assumed that was you."

Her eyes twinkled with humor. "Nope. That was my aunt's full name. My full name is Rebecca Elizabeth Arrington. And I don't have a Honey Bee." A smile spread across her face. "At least, I didn't until now."

"No." He held up a hand. "Get that thought out of your head immediately, Rebecca. I am not your Honey Bee. What happened just now was a mistake. A mistake that won't happen again."

He got off the bed and walked into the bathroom, slamming the door behind him. Once he disposed of the condom, he stood at the sink and tried to get a grip on his careening emotions. He felt guilty as hell for taking her virginity and pissed that she'd used him to get rid of it. Not only had she gotten a fantasy into her head about being a submissive, she'd also gotten a fantasy in her head about Mason being her Honey Bee. But Honey Bee and Lucy had had a love affair. And Mason didn't believe in love.

He needed to make that perfectly clear.

But when he stepped out of the bathroom, he found Becky fast asleep. She slept on her stomach with her face pressed into a pillow and one foot dangling off the bed. It was hard to look away from the perfection of her body, the long toned legs and curvy butt that still carried the prints of his hand. The sight made him feel even guiltier, and he lifted the quilt she'd taken from his house and pulled it over her.

He was tucking it under her shoulder when her eyes fluttered open. They widened before recognition settled in the deep sky-blue depths. Before he could straighten, she grabbed his hand and pressed his knuckles to her lips.

"Stay with me, Honey Bee . . . please."

Mason stayed.

"Valentine had done something stupid. She'd fallen in love with a man who could never be happy with a soiled dove."

❦

CHAPTER TWELVE

THE SIGHT OF MASON RIDING toward her on Ghost Rider left Becky feeling surprised and more than a little breathless. She'd learned a lot about him in the last week: He was an amazing cook. He had a soft spot for animals. He didn't mind getting his hands dirty helping out on the ranch. And he knew his way around a bedroom—although it had taken some doing to get him there.

Every night, he would list the reasons why they shouldn't be sleeping together, and every night she would sneak into the guestroom and change his mind. If he had locked the door, she would've believed him. But the door was never locked. And last night, it had only taken her dropping her nightshirt for him to reach for her.

He claimed he was a dominant, but since the first spanking, he'd never once gotten rough with her. Instead, he treated her like spun glass. Like he was worried that if he handled her too roughly she would break. She intended to disabuse him of that notion.

She watched as he galloped across the open pasture toward her. He handled the high-spirited horse better than she did. When he reached the herd of cattle she and the ranch hands were taking to another pasture, he easily guided Ghost Rider through the herd and to where she sat on her bay cutting horse, Jinx.

"You need to tell me where a city boy like you learned to ride," she teased.

"My stepdad Dan had a ranch."

Yet another stepdad. In the last week, she'd learned that Mason's stepdad Bill had taught him to fish. Stepdad Greg had taught him football. And stepdad Donald was the reason he'd chosen to study the law. Becky was starting to get a clearer picture of Mason's childhood. It had been far from idyllic. While he never spoke badly about his stepfathers, the revolving door of daddies had to have left some major insecurities in a kid. Which probably explained Mason's need for control.

"It's three o'clock," he said.

"You rode all this way to give me the time?"

"I rode all this way because you didn't eat breakfast today. And if you're not going to eat breakfast, you need to eat lunch." He glanced at his watch. "It's 3:01."

She bit back a smile. "Thank you, Big Ben. But if you remember, there was a good reason why I didn't eat breakfast this morning."

His mouth tipped down at the corners as if she'd just called him a bad name, instead of brought up their lovemaking. "That shouldn't have happened. Especially if it made you skip breakfast.

Now what's your excuse for not eating lunch?"

"We have to move this herd to a pasture with more water. I don't have time to worry about lunch."

He sighed. "I get that you want Zane to be proud of the way you take care of the ranch while he's gone, but I don't think he'll be happy if you die of starvation." He used Zane as an excuse for watching out for her all the time. But she no longer believed him. He hadn't liked her when they first met, but he liked her now. He cared if she ate breakfast and lunch. He cared if she had a stalker. And he cared if she reached orgasm.

She had started to care about him too. He made her happy. Happier than she'd been in a long time. She loved working the ranch, but she'd always felt like something was missing from her life, which is why she'd dated so many guys. She had been trying to fill the void. But not one guy had filled that void . . . until now. Mason completed her. He made her world perfect.

Unable to stop herself, she leaned out of the saddle and kissed him right on the mouth. The look that entered his eyes was surprise mixed with something she couldn't read. "What are you doing?" he asked, glancing over to Jess and the other two ranch hands.

"I was just thanking you for worrying about me. But I can't leave until we get this herd to the pasture."

He didn't look happy, but he conceded. "Fine. But as soon as we get them there, you're coming with me."

She smiled. "Of course. I love to come with

you."

It didn't take them long to get the herd to the smaller pasture. Once the gate was closed, she expected Mason to head back to the ranch. Instead, he led her in the opposite direction. "I thought we'd eat lunch at my house for a change. How do sandwiches and some of Ms. Marble's brownies sound?"

They sounded good, but not nearly as good as making love in Lucy and Honey Bee's brass bed. She shot him a sassy look before she set her boot heels to her horse.

"Race you!"

Ghost Rider was a faster horse than Jinx, but Becky had size and experience on her side. She leaned close to Jinx's neck and gave her free rein. She glanced behind her only once and was surprised to see Mason a lot closer than she'd expected. They were neck and neck by the time they reached his house.

She laughed as she reined in the horse. "I won by a nose. And as the victor, I should get the spoils."

Mason swung down from Ghost Rider and looped the reins to the porch railing. "And exactly what did you have in mind?" He took her reins and tied Jinx before reaching for her.

Once she was in his arms, she wrapped her hands around his neck. "I want you to stop treating me like I'm breakable. In case you haven't figured it out, I'm tough, Mason. I can handle things getting a little rough. In fact, I like it."

His eyes turned dark and smoldering. Without a word, he swept her up in his arms and carried her into the house. He laid her on the brass bed, then pulled her t-shirt over her head. He walked to the closet, and when he came back he carried two silk ties. He sat next to her on the bed and studied her with those dark, penetrating eyes.

"Are you sure?" he asked in a low whisper that sent shivers of excitement down her spine. She nodded, but that wasn't good enough. "Say it, Rebecca. Tell me what you want."

She swallowed. "I want you to tie me up."

Their gazes locked as he took her hands and expertly looped one of the ties around her wrists. Once they were lashed together, he lifted them over her head and tied them to the brass head-board. He tightened it with a hard yank that caused her to jump. He tipped his head. "Whenever you want me to stop, I will. Do you want me to stop?"

She shook her head, then remembered that she needed to answer. "No. I trust you." It was the truth. She did trust him. More than she'd ever trusted a man before.

He nodded before he took the other tie and tied it over her eyes. When it was tight, he brushed a kiss on her lips. A few seconds later, she heard a boot clunk to the floor, then the other. The mattress shifted as he got up, and she heard snaps pop and the sound of clothes being discarded. Her boots were lifted and tugged off. She felt a brush of his warm fingers on her calves as he slipped her socks down. She thought her jeans would be harder to take off, but Mason proved to be an expert at removing women's clothing. Once he had the button open and the zipper down, he issued an order.

"Hold tight to the tie and lift your hips." As soon as she did, he pulled the jeans off.

A long stretch of silence ensued, and she could picture him standing naked at the foot of the bed looking at her. Desire washed over her in waves. The waves swelled when the mattress dipped and his warm, muscled body settled next to her. His fingertips trailed along the sensitive underside of her arm until he reached the strap of her bra. He followed it down, and his hand encompassed her breast in a gentle squeeze before he roughly tugged down the lacy cup. He did the same to the other cup until both breasts were exposed and pushed up by the lace and underwire.

His breath fell heavy against her ear. "You want it rough, Rebecca?" When she only moaned, he leaned closer. "Say it."

"Yes." The word came out on a croak of desire and ended on a surprised moan when he pinched her nipple hard.

It hurt, but it was a good hurt. He followed it up with a deep, suckling kiss. He repeated the process again and again until both nipples were wonderfully abused and mind-blowingly aroused. Her hips undulated against the mattress, and she wondered if she could reach orgasm from just having her breasts touched.

But before she could find out the answer to that question, his hand moved down her body. Her stomach muscles quivered as his hot fingers dipped beneath her panties. He separated the folds and gently stroked her swollen clitoris. Once. Twice. Three times. Then he pinched her. That was all it took to send her over the edge of an amazing climax.

Before the tremors had completely stopped, he had her panties off and a pillow under her hips. This time he held nothing back. He knelt between her legs and entered her with a hard thrust. His growl of pleasure had desire swelling in her once again, and she lifted her hips to meet each of his thrusts until they both broke through to a climax. They came together in a groan of shared satisfaction. He ended up sprawled on top of her, his heavy weight pressing her into the mattress. But she didn't mind. If her hands had been free, she would've held him closer.

He finally lifted his head and removed her blindfold. She blinked him into focus to find more than a little concern in his beautiful brown eyes. "Are you okay?"

She gave him a sassy look. "From a few pinches? You're going to have to get rougher than that to scare this girl off." She nipped at his shoulder. "Now feed me, Honey Bee. Your queen is starving!"

They ate turkey and provolone sandwiches in bed. It seemed so wicked to be completely naked in broad daylight with Mason sprawled at the foot of the bed, alternating bites of his sandwich with nibbles on her toes.

"So who's your favorite Tender Heart character?" she asked between bites. "I'm guessing the gunslinger Dax Davenport."

He wiggled his dark eyebrows. "Because I'm such a villain." He nipped at her instep until she giggled. He didn't laugh, but there was a sparkle of happiness in his eyes. "I don't know if I could pick one favorite. I liked Rory for his cool head. Duke for his tenacity. The youngest Arrington, Johnny, for his wit and charm. He certainly charmed feisty Daisy." He glanced at her. "I'm assuming Daisy McNeil is your favorite."

She finished off the last of her sandwich. He had remembered the sour pickles and mustard that she liked. The man paid attention to the details. "I like Daisy, but she isn't my favorite. My favorite is Valentine Clemens."

He halted with her foot halfway to his mouth. "The prostitute?"

"She was not a prostitute. She was a saloon girl."

"What do you think a saloon girl did? Your aunt even called her a soiled dove."

She couldn't help defending her favorite character. "Well, she wasn't a prostitute after she came to Tender Heart. She was the one who organized the women and made sure the men didn't take advantage of them before they were lawfully wed. And she made Lance Butler fall in love with her."

The smile left Mason's eyes. "You can't make a person love you. They either do or they don't."

Hoping to bring back the sparkle of happiness, she teased, "Maybe I'll prove you wrong."

A dark cloud came over his features. "That's not going to happen, Rebecca. I don't do love."

"What do you mean? Of course you do love. Everyone loves someone and is loved by someone." She paused. "I don't mean me and you . . . but someone."

He dropped her foot and sat up, setting the rest of his sandwich on the nightstand. "We better go."

He started to stand, but she couldn't let him leave on such a sad note. She didn't know what his mother had done to him to make him feel like love wasn't an option for him. All she knew was that he needed a good hug. And that's exactly what she gave him. She wrapped herself around him from behind, hooking her legs around his waist and her arms around his shoulders. Then she pressed her cheek to his back and squeezed. There was a moment when she thought he was going to fight her. Instead, he just sat there as if he were stunned. And that broke her heart even more.

They stayed that way until a car door slammed out front. It was followed by a booming voice she immediately recognized.

"Rebecca Elizabeth Arrington!"

"Holy crap!" She scrambled off the bed. "It's my daddy."

"Shit." Mason jumped up and grabbed her clothes, tossing them to her before he searched for his own. A pounding on the front door made her move even faster. But her hands were shaking so badly, she couldn't get her bra hooked. When Mason finished dressing, he came over and helped her.

"Deep breath," he said as he hooked her bra. "We'll just tell him we went out riding and stopped here for lunch."

She nodded. "Okay, but if he doesn't believe you, run for the hills. My daddy has a mean right hook. . . and a Smith & Wesson."

But as it turned out, her father was too intent on yelling at her to pay much attention to Mason.

"What the hell do you think you're doing, lit-tle girl?" His face was red beneath the brim of his Stetson. He looked just like her brother—tall, handsome, and blond, but with a little silver at the temples. "When Zane is gone from the ranch, it's your responsibility to be there in case of a prob-lem. Not gallivanting all over the countryside. I knew I shouldn't have trusted you with the job. You're still too young and flighty."

Becky was about to argue the point when Mason stepped up.

"I respectfully disagree, sir. Becky is one of the best ranch mangers I've ever seen—male or female. Except for a brief time today, she's been working non-stop while Zane's been gone and doing a damned good job."

Becky was completely blindsided. No one had ever stood up for her with her daddy. Not her mama. Not Zane. Not any of her boyfriends. Peo-ple didn't go against Dale Arrington. But Mason had. And he'd done it for her. At that moment, she did something really stupid.

She fell in love.

"'She's leaving,' Etta Jenkins said. 'And you can't let her go. Of all the women, Valentine is the one who will make the best wife.' It was funny, but Lance had been thinking the same thing."

❦

CHAPTER THIRTEEN

MASON DIDN'T STAY AT THE Arrington's ranch house that night. He went back to his place and spent a sleepless night thinking about Becky. The worst possible thing had happened: She had fallen in love with him. She hadn't told him, but he didn't need words to know the truth. It was there in her eyes when they rode back to Earhart Ranch. Every time he glanced over, he saw a tenderness that made his chest feel like it was being squeezed in a vise.

He had come to Bliss looking for Tender Heart. And he had found it in a feisty woman with eyes the color of twilight and a heart the size of Texas. Becky was the personification of the series. Inside her was the wild and untamed spirit of the Earharts and the single-minded determination of the mail-order brides. She was a free spirit who believed she could accomplish all her dreams and find her happily-ever-after. And Mason believed that she would. But not with him. Not with someone who was so jaded and lost. She needed someone as innocent as she was. Someone who still believed in love.

Unfortunately, once Becky set her sights on something, she didn't give up easily. The Reed property was a perfect example. She still hadn't given up on buying it. And now that she'd set her sights on Mason, he didn't doubt that she would do everything in her power to get him and the ranch too. Which was why he had no choice but to leave Bliss. Once he was gone, she would forget about him and move on. She would find another Honey Bee who deserved her love.

He finally fell asleep as the light of dawn crept through the window. When he woke, it was late afternoon. He got up and fixed himself something to eat, then showered, dressed, and parked. He had just zipped his suitcase when he heard the whinny of a horse. Only a few seconds later, the front door opened and boot heels clicked against the floor. He recognized the determined stride immediately and wasn't surprised when Becky appeared in the doorway.

She wore her customary cowboy hat, t-shirt, jeans, and boots. Her hair hung in a tangle around her shoulders as if she'd ridden hard to get to him. She lifted the cat she carried in her arms. "I found Furball on the porch. He must've followed you back here." Her eyes landed on the open suitcase on the bed before piercing him with heartbreaking blue. "You're leaving."

He reached out as if to scratch the cat, but let his hand drop. "I need to get back to Austin."

She cradled the cat closer as tears shimmered in her eyes. Tears that made Mason feel as if he were suffocating. "Don't lie. You don't need to get back to Austin. You're leaving because I broke the rules." She swallowed hard. "You're leaving because I fell in love with you."

Hearing the words from her lips was a mixture of heaven and hell. They eased an ache down deep inside, and at the same time created a new one. This new one was much deeper than the last. It was a struggle not to pull her into his arms and try to find relief from the pain. Instead, he tightened his hands into fists.

"I'm the one who broke the rules, Rebecca. I knew you didn't know how to play my game, and yet I made love to you anyway."

She stared at him. "Made love? I thought it was just sex."

He hadn't realized the slip until she pointed it out. Now, it was too late to deny it. "Not with you," he said. "It wasn't just sex with you."

She blinked back the tears. "But you're still leaving."

It wasn't a question, but he answered it anyway. "You don't want someone as screwed up as I am. You want someone without all my baggage."

The tears dried up as quickly as they had appeared. Suddenly, she was the feisty Becky he'd first met. "Don't you dare tell me what I want, Mason Granger! Or what I need. I have enough people trying to control my life. My mama thinks I need a husband to tame my wild ways. My daddy thinks I need to remain his little girl forever. And my brother thinks I need to run the ranch his way.

Well, I don't need any of those things. I want to own my own ranch with a man who treats me like a woman and an equal. I don't give a damn what kind of baggage he has. Baggage is something you choose to carry with you. If you're tired of carrying it, all you have to do is let it go."

He smiled sadly. "Unless you can't."

She stared at him for what felt like forever. It was easy to read the disappointment in her eyes. A disappointment that made him feel gutted. "I should've learned from Lucy," she said in quavering voice. "I should've learned never to fall in love with a Honey Bee. Because while they can make sweet honey, they can never stay." A tear rolled down her cheek, and she quickly brushed it away. "Goodbye, Mason." She walked out with the cat still cradled in her arms.

He waited for the front door to slam before he whispered. "Goodbye, Rebecca."

Once she was gone, he got his briefcase and pulled out the deed to the ranch. It didn't take long to sign it over to Becky. He realized that he was trying to assuage his guilt. But he also truly believed that the ranch should belong to someone who understood the history. He left the deed and the keys to the front door in the center of the bed before he packed his Range Rover. He placed his mother's urn next to him in the front seat. Becky was right. He needed to let go of some baggage.

The field in front of the little white chapel looked as wilted as Mason felt, and he wasted no time opening the urn and pouring out his mother's ashes. There was no wind to catch them. They settled into the sun-parched ground like tiny gray feathers. He stared down at them and tried to come up with a prayer. But all that came to him was a wish. The same wish he'd had all his life.

"Be happy, Mother."

He started back to his car, but stopped when he saw Ms. Marble standing just inside the line of trees. She wore her usual floral dress, wide-brimmed bonnet, and white gloves. She carried a bouquet of pink roses. He didn't doubt that she'd watched him pour out his mother's ashes. Her eagle eyes were pinned on the urn he held under one arm. Although she didn't say anything about it.

"Walk me around to the cemetery," she said. "I'm worried I'm going to break an ankle with all these gopher holes." He took her arm and allowed her to lead him. On the way passed the spot where he'd spread his mother's ashes, she pulled out a pink rose from the dozen in her arms and leaned down to place it on the ground. He had to fight back the tears that threatened.

"She loved pink."

"A lot of women do," Ms. Marble said as they continued to a worn path that wound around the church. "I never much cared for it myself. But it was Lucy's favorite color."

He glanced down at the flowers. "Those are for Lucy Arrington? Her grave site is here?"

She glanced at him with surprise. "I didn't take you for a Tender Heart fan."

"My mom used to read the books to me when I was a kid. It's the only time I ever remember her showing any genuine emotion. She'd laugh and cry right along with the characters." He paused.

"I guess that's why I thought she might find happiness here. She certainly didn't find it while she was living."

Ms. Marble didn't say anything until they reached the small cemetery beneath a stand of huge oak trees. She stopped at the gate and turned to him. "And what about you? Have you found happiness?"

He didn't have to search too hard for the answer. He had found happiness. He'd found it with Becky. But just because he'd found it didn't mean he could hold onto it. His mother had found happiness with each of the men she'd married, but it had never lasted. And his stepfathers had become the casualties in her quest for love. Mason wasn't willing for Becky to be one of his.

He opened the gate and held it for Ms. Marble. "Maybe I'm like my mother. Maybe I won't ever find enduring happiness."

Ms. Marble snorted. "That's bullshit." The word surprised him. "Happiness doesn't elude people. People elude happiness. I should know. I thought I could only truly be happy with one man. And when he died, I thought that was the end of my happiness. I was so convinced of this that I wasted years withholding love from my dear David." She poked him in the chest with a gloved finger. "Don't make the same mistake I made."

She walked past him into the cemetery. He followed more slowly. Was she right? Was his fear of being like his mother causing him to make a huge mistake? He was still mulling over the question when he found Ms. Marble placing the roses on a gravestone shaped like an open book. Tears were in her eyes as she straightened and stared at the name engraved in the stone.

"Even though we were three years apart, Lucy and I were good friends. My daddy was the foreman of the Arrington Ranch, and as little girls, we used to come here to the chapel and play. We would use the lacy doilies her grandmother crocheted as veils and pick flowers from the fields for our bouquets." She smiled as she looked down at the gravestone. "Of course, Lucy was always the more imaginative. While I just had an ordinary cowboy as a groom, Lucy's groom would be a Persian prince or a Russian Cossack. She dreamed of going to all those exotic places."

"Why didn't she?"

Her smile faded. "Life has a way of changing your dreams. After she started writing the series, she became reclusive. She didn't want to go anywhere outside of Bliss. She wouldn't even do signings. When she got sick, all she wanted was to finish the last book."

"And you think she did?"

She glanced at him. "Lucy could do anything she set her mind to."

Mason paused for only a moment. "Except make Honey Bee fall in love with her."

Ms. Marble's eyes flickered with something before she looked back at the gravestone. She released her breath in a quivery sigh. "You can't make someone fall in love. Either they do or they don't. Although sometimes they do and they're too stubborn to admit it." She glanced at him, her eyes as intense and piercing as ever. "When I saw that urn in your kitchen window, I knew you had some unresolved issues with your mother. Otherwise you wouldn't have been carrying her around. But now that you've put her to rest, it's time to release her and move on. And I'm not talking about back to Austin."

"Who told you I was going back to Austin?"

"I stopped by your house on my way here to drop off some cookies. I looked in the bedroom and found something very interesting on your bed."

Mason didn't even attempt to play dumb. "Becky and I have become friends. Since I won't be coming back, I thought she should have the ranch."

Ms. Marble's almost invisible eyebrows lifted. "Deeding over an entire ranch seems like a pretty big gift for a friend." When he didn't say anything, she reached out and squeezed his arm. "I can't keep you from leaving, Mason. But don't take too long to figure out your mistake. Becky's not the type of girl who'll wait forever."

"Valentine couldn't have been more surprised when Lance waltzed into the boardinghouse, scooped her up in his arms, and carried her out. 'I don't care about the past,' he said. 'All I care about is the future. And mine is going to be bleak if you're not by my side.'"

☙

CHAPTER FOURTEEN

BECKY'S BIRTHDAY PARTY *WAS* A surprise. There were no pink decorations. No string quartet. No china or crystal. No seared salmon. And no exclusive hotel. The barn was decorated with twinkle lights that draped from the hayloft over a wooden dance floor. A long table ran through the center of the barn with covered hay bales for seats and groups of candles in mason jars as centerpieces. Barbecue smoke scented the air. And a country band was set up to the left of the dance floor and was playing "Happy Birthday" as she and her daddy rode up. Her daddy had worked hard at keeping her busy all day. It hadn't been easy to slip away and see Mason.

Becky had known something was wrong when he'd left the ranch the night before without saying goodbye. And when she saw the suitcase, it didn't take a genius to figure out why he was leaving.

He didn't do love. It was too bad that her heart hadn't listened. It felt like it had been trampled by a hundred head of cattle, and it took everything she had to keep a smile on her face as Zane broke away from her family and friends.

"Happy birthday, baby sister." He went to help her down, but stopped when he saw the cat draped over her lap. "A birthday present?"

She cradled the cat in one arm as she swung down from the horse. "Just a stray."

She had kept the cat with her since leaving Mason's, and Furball hadn't seemed to mind. Once on the ground, she set the cat down and hugged Zane. She held on a little too tightly.

"Don't tell me you missed me," her brother teased as he hugged her back.

"Not even a little." She drew away. "Now why did you leave your honeymoon early? Please don't tell me it had to do with my birthday."

"You know I can't stay away from the ranch for long. And Carly wasn't about to stay away from the diner. She fretted the entire time over Dirk screwing up her recipes."

"I'm sure she didn't fret the entire time."

He grinned. "I refuse to talk about my honeymoon with my little sister. Now let me take this beast to the stable so you can go greet your guests."

For the next hour, she ignored the gaping hole in her heart and forced a smile while she thanked people for coming to celebrate her birthday. Her mama was the only one who knew something wasn't right.

"Please don't tell me you got your monthly,

Rebecca Elizabeth," she whispered as she led Becky to the hay bale at the head of the table. "Your face is as pale as death."

"I'm fine, Mama. I'm just a little tired, is all."

"Which is exactly why I didn't want you spending the day with your daddy. The man could work a farm mule into the ground. What happened to Mason Granger? Zane said he was going to keep you busy."

Just hearing his name made Becky feel like bursting into tears. She swallowed hard. "Mason had to go back to Austin."

"That's a shame. Zane speaks so highly of him, I was looking forward to meeting him." Her mama waited for her to sit down before she reached out and pinched her cheeks. "Really, Rebecca Elizabeth, you need to start wearing blush."

The dinner passed in a blur. Becky took very little from the platters of ribs, chicken, and pulled pork that were passed her way. When the cake was brought out, she needed two breaths to blow out the twenty-five candles that blazed on top. She was only able to choke down one bite before she had to excuse herself. Inside her room, she finally gave in to the tears. Once they started, they were hard to stop. She was still sobbing in her pillow when someone tapped on the door.

She quickly sat up and grabbed a tissue. "I'll be right out, Mama. I was just applying some blush."

"It's not your mama. It's Ms. Marble. Can I come in?"

There was no way Becky could say no to the woman. She blotted her eyes and blew her nose before she got up and opened the door.

"Hi, Ms. Marble." She plastered on a smile. "I wanted to thank you for the cake. Strawberry has always been my favorite."

"You're more than welcome." Ms. Marble said. "But I didn't come here looking for gratitude. I wanted to make sure you don't give up on that boy."

"Excuse me?"

Ms. Marble sent her a pointed look. "Don't you play dumb with me, Becky Arrington. You tried that in first grade when you didn't want to finish your math homework. It didn't work then, and it's not going to work now. You know exactly what boy I'm talking about. Believe me, I realize that it's hard to love a stubborn man. But you can't give up on them and leave them to their own bull-headedness. If every woman did that, there would be very few marriages and lots of lost men."

Tears dripped down Becky's cheeks. "But Mason doesn't do love."

"That's flat-out nonsense. He tries to act like he's tough, but that man is as sensitive and loving as the day is long. And spreading his mother's ashes at the little white chapel proves it."

"He spread his mother's ashes at the chapel?"

Ms. Marble nodded, causing the brim of her summer bonnet to bounce. "He wanted to give his mother the perfect resting place, and a man who worries about his dead mother's happiness is a man who loves deeply."

"Maybe he just doesn't love me."

The look in Ms. Marble's eyes was pure exasperation. "Why would he deed you the Reed ranch if he doesn't love you?"

It was too much for Becky to absorb. She stared at Ms. Marble with shock . . . and hope.

"Just as I thought," Ms. Marble said. "I figured you didn't know about the deed when I saw you moping around the party. I would love to continue this conversation, but we don't have a lot of time." She took Becky's arm and pulled her out into the hallway and toward the front door. "You need to get to Austin and convince Mason he can't live without you."

Becky grabbed her cowboy hat off the hook by the door. "But how do I do that? You're right. Mason is stubborn and bullheaded, and he's made up his mind that he doesn't deserve love."

"I'm sure you'll figure out something. You were named after your great-aunt and the same determined genes run in your body as ran in Lucy's." Ms. Marble pulled her out onto the porch. The party was in full swing, which presented another problem.

"What about my party?" she said. "Mama will kill me if I leave."

"You leave your mama to me." Ms. Marble gave her a hug and a pat on the back. "You just go get Mason and get him back to Bliss. I've grown quite attached to that boy."

Becky drew back and smiled. "So have I." She helped Ms. Marble down the porch steps before she headed for her truck. But once she reached for the door handle, doubt started to kick in. What if Ms. Marble was wrong? What if Mason had deeded her the ranch out of guilt? If that were the case, she'd end up making a fool of herself in Austin. But would she rather be a fool and know for certain, or would she rather stay here and never know the truth? The decision was an easy one.

She opened the door and climbed in. It wasn't until she'd slammed the door and reached for the ignition button that she noticed the man crouched on the floor.

"Rich?"

He smiled a creepy smile as he pointed a wicked-looking knife at her. "And here I thought you had forgotten me, Becky."

☾

Mason should've headed to Austin right after Ms. Marble left. Instead, he went inside the chapel. The setting sun filtered through the stained-glass windows, casting a kaleidoscope of colors over the rows of pews. He sat in the same pew Becky had slept in, his mother's urn sitting next to him. He didn't pray. He just thought about what Ms. Marble had said.

Was she right? Did people make the choice to be happy? Had his mother wrongly blamed all her husbands for her unhappiness when she had been the one responsible—when she had been the one who had rejected happiness? Rejected love?

He should've realized the truth at the funeral when all his stepfathers had talked about their love for his mom. The love had been there. She'd just refused to accept it and be happy. And Mason had made the same mistake. He'd held women at arm's length, using them only in sexual scenarios that he set up so there was no chance he could be hurt.

Until Becky.

Becky refused to be held at arm's length. She slipped beneath all his defenses and wiggled her way right into his cold heart and filled it with joy. Now all he had to do was accept it. All he had to do was go after his own happiness and hold on tight.

It was dark by the time he got to the Earhart Ranch. It looked like the entire town had come out for Becky's birthday. Couples shuffled around the dance floor while other people clustered in groups talking and laughing. Mason looked for Becky, but it was hard to spot anyone in the dim glow of the stringed lights. He finally found Zane standing by the fence of the paddock.

A big smile broke over Zane's face when he saw him. "I thought you weren't going to make it." He grabbed Mason's hand and gave it a welcoming shake.

"Sorry," Mason said. "There was some business I needed to attend to." He glanced around. "Have you seen Becky?"

"No, but I'm sure she's here somewhere. I wanted to thank you for keeping an eye on her while I was gone. According to everyone I've talked with, she did a damn good job of keeping things running smoothly."

"She can handle the ranch just fine by herself, Zane. I think you and your dad don't give her enough credit for that."

Zane looked surprised for only a second before he grinned and shook his head. "I didn't think it would happen to Iceman Granger, but it looks like my sister has you under her spell."

Mason didn't try to deny it. "From the moment I met her." He looked at the spot where her truck was usually parked. "Is her truck in the garage?"

"No. It was parked right there only a few minutes ago." Zane laughed. "Only Becky would run off from her own birthday party. Mama's gonna kill her." He sent Mason a pointed look. "So you like Becky?"

It was still an uncomfortable subject, but Mason figured he needed to get used to it. "I love her."

While Zane stared at him with surprise, an attractive middle-aged woman walked up. Her brown-and-gold-threaded hair was too much like Becky's to be a coincidence. And her directness was a dead giveaway. "I'm going to make a guess and say you're Mason. Would you like to explain why you couldn't entertain my daughter today? Especially when it appears that you didn't go to Austin."

"I'm sorry, ma'am. I planned to return to Austin, but then realized what a mistake that would be."

Mrs. Arrington arched an eyebrow. "I admire a man who can admit when he's making a mistake. Of course, from what Ms. Marble just told me, I don't think my daughter would've let you do that. Rebecca left for Austin to bring you back."

Mason couldn't help the smile that spread across his face. No matter what he said or did, Becky wasn't going to give up on him. That was the best feeling in the world.

"If you'll excuse me, Mrs. Arrington. I'd better call her. She'll be fit to be tied if she gets to Austin and I'm not there."

Zane laughed and slapped him on the back. "You do know my hellion of a sister."

Mrs. Arrington shot a stern look at her son. "She's not a hellion, Zane. She's just strong willed. Now if you'll excuse me, I need to stop your father from eating any more barbecue or the spices will keep him up all night."

Once she was gone, Mason was about to pull out his phone when Dirk walked up. "Hey, man, how's that air conditioner working?"

"Great. Thanks for helping me out with it. I'd like your opinion on some other improvements I plan on making to the house, but right now I need to call Becky."

"I just saw her in town."

Mason lowered his phone. "In town?" That was the opposite direction from Austin.

"Yeah. We ran out of cake so Carly sent me to the diner to get some of Ms. Marble's pies, and on the way back, I passed Becky and that guy she used to date. Ryan? Richard?"

A tingle of fear ran up Mason's spine. "Rich?"

Dirk nodded. "That's the guy. He was sitting right there next to her when she drove past me."

"Something isn't right," Zane said. "I know for damn sure that Rich wasn't invited to the party. And Becky wouldn't leave with him willingly. She hates the guy."

Mason was thinking the same thing and didn't hesitate to dial 911. Both Dirk and Zane were listening when he gave the operator Rich's address and the details about his stalking, and when he hung up and headed for his SUV, they were right there with him. By the time they reached Rich's trailer, Mason had told Zane and Dirk the full story. Neither seemed happy that Mason had kept the information to himself, but he couldn't worry about that right now. He was too worried about Becky. If anything happened to her, he didn't know what he would do.

He turned off the lights and engine and rolled to a stop in front of the trailer. "We need to keep our cool," he said to himself as much as Zane and Dirk. "I don't want him getting upset and hurting Becky."

"If he hurts her, he's dead," Zane said between clenched teeth. "But you're right. We need to keep our cool. Then, after she's safe, I'm beating the bastard senseless."

"After me." Dirk opened his door.

Not if Mason got to him first.

As it turned out, not one of the three men got a chance to beat Rich senseless. They stepped into the trailer to find Rich sprawled facedown on the floor in front of a dilapidated couch. Becky sat on the couch rubbing her knuckles. When she saw Mason, she smiled as if she'd expected him.

"It's about time, Granger."

While Zane and Dirk grabbed Rich's arms and dragged him out the door to await the sheriff, he walked over and pulled Becky into his arms. "Are you okay? Did he hurt you?"

"I'm fine." Relief had him squeezing her a little too tightly, and she quickly added, "as long as you don't crack a rib." He started to release her, but she tightened her arms around his waist and snuggled her head into his chest. "So are you ready to tell me why you deeded me the ranch?"

He breathed in her familiar scent of fresh-cut pastures and everything he'd come to love. "Because you wanted it."

She drew back. "And since when do you give me what I want?"

"Since I fell totally and completely in love with you and realized that I want to spend the rest of my life giving you what you want."

Her beautiful blue eyes glistened with tears. "Even if I want a small wedding in a little white chapel?"

He didn't even hesitate. "Even then."

A big smile spread over her face. He planned to work hard to keep that smile there always. "Okay, but it's going to be pretty embarrassing to be married to a cat guy."

"Deal with it." He kissed her.

"It felt like a dream being married in a little white chapel to a tall, dark, and handsome man who promised to love, protect, and cherish her for the rest of his life. And if was a dream, Valentine never wanted to wake up."

☾

CHAPTER FIFTEEN

BECKY HAD ESCAPED PINK FOR her birthday, but her mama made up for it on her wedding day. The little white chapel was an explosion of pink flowers, pink tulle, and pink ribbons. Even Furball had a pink bow around his neck. But the cat didn't seem to mind. He pranced down the aisle on the leash Carly held like he was the bride.

Becky's sister-in-law looked like a fairy in her pink confection of a bridesmaid's dress. And if Carly looked like a fairy, Gracie looked like a princess. A beautiful princess who was walking down the aisle on her own.

Gracie had surprised Becky just that morning when she arrived at the ranch without a wheelchair. She still needed to use a walker, but Gracie walking was the best wedding present Becky could've asked for.

"You can still change your mind, little girl."

She glanced over at her daddy, who looked

extremely handsome in his tux. He also looked sad. He might be bossy, but she knew he loved her and was going to miss ordering her around. She straightened his bow tie. "I'm not going to change my mind."

"Well, you should. You've known the man for less than a month and now you're going to spend the rest of your life with him. That's just plain crazy."

Becky leaned in and gave him a kiss on the cheek. "You know I've always been a little crazy, Daddy."

The wedding march started. Her daddy rolled his eyes and held out his arm. "Then let's get this show on the road."

But when she moved into the aisle and saw the groom, she started to second-guess her decision to get married so quickly. With his dark hair slicked back and dressed in an expensive designer tux, Mason looked like he belonged on the cover of a magazine. He did not look like he belonged in a simple white chapel getting ready to marry a stubborn cowgirl.

But then his dark eyes met hers. And in them she saw love and happiness. The same love and happiness that filled her heart. She released her daddy's arm and strode straight down the aisle to the man she loved with all her heart. He laughed, something he'd done a lot of lately.

"So I guess you're ready to be my bride."

She lifted her chin and sent him a saucy look. "I was born ready."

The ceremony didn't take long, and before she knew it, she was Mrs. Mason Samuel Granger.

They left the church, only to walk a few yards away to the tent that had been set up in the open field. The tent was as pink as the chapel. But regardless of the decorations, her mama had done a wonderful job.

Salmon was on the menu, but so were steak and barbecue. Ms. Marble had made the five-tier wedding cake with a chocolate layer just for Mason and a strawberry one for Becky. And the country music and margarita fountain didn't stop flowing . . . until the rainstorm hit.

After weeks of heat, it wasn't a curse as much as a blessing. The people of Bliss didn't hesitate to enjoy it. Disregarding their wedding finery, they walked right out of the tent and into the cooling summer rain where they danced around like a bunch of crazy Texans.

Mason and Becky were right in the middle of the mayhem. Although after only one dance, Becky's dress became so heavy she could barely kick up her pink boots. Seeing her dilemma, Mason swept her up in his arms and carried her to his SUV. When they drove under the new scrolled-metal gate of the Double G Ranch, Becky couldn't help feeling a little guilty.

"I hope Gracie wasn't lying when she said she wasn't upset about us living in the house and starting our own ranch."

Mason brought her hand to his lips and pressed a kiss to her knuckles. "When I talked to her at the reception, she told me it was never her dream to live here. She just wanted to make sure Lucy's secret was kept and the diary remained in the house." He winked at her. "I didn't tell her that you snuck the diary out weeks ago."

Becky laughed. "Right. And exactly when did I have time to do that? Every time I've been at the house, I can't seem to get out of your bed."

She thought he would make a suggestive remark, instead he looked stunned. "You didn't take the diary?"

Her heart sank. "You're not kidding? It's gone? Lucy's diary is gone?"

Mason parked in front of the porch. "Now calm down. I'm sure—"

She didn't let him finish before she jumped out and hurried through the rain. It was dark inside the house, but she didn't waste time turning on a light. She knelt in the corner and removed the boards, then reached down between the floor joists for the wooden box. She opened it to find the diary all safe and sound.

Mason strode into the room. "I realize you're upset, Rebecca. And I take full responsibility." He walked to the nightstand and switched on the lamp. "I should've put it back in the floor. I just didn't think anyone else knew about—" He turned and froze when he saw the diary in her hands. "It's there? But someone took it from under my pillow, and when I looked in the floor, the box was empty. Now why would someone take it and then return it?"

She shrugged. "I don't know. Maybe once they read it, they decided to keep Lucy's secret too."

Mason helped her to her feet. "Well, we're not going to take another chance. We'll need to figure out a more secure place to keep it before we go back to Austin to close down my practice." He took the diary from her and set it on the nightstand before he pulled her into his arms. "Are you sure you're okay with being away from Bliss for a couple months?"

She hooked her arms around his neck. "Are you sure you're okay with moving here forever and being a rancher's husband? Being an attorney in a small town won't be nearly as exciting as being a divorce lawyer in a big city. People don't get a lot of divorces here."

He hugged her tighter. "I'm counting on that. Whether you like it or not, Mrs. Granger, you're stuck with me."

"There's no other honeybee I'd rather be stuck with." She smiled wickedly. "Now get your silk tie . . . please."

Here's a sneak peek at the next book in
Katie Lane's
TENDER HEART TEXAS
series!

❦

FALLING FOR A COWBOY'S SMILE

is out September 2017!

IT WAS HARD WORK BEING the sweetest girl in Bliss, Texas.

Sometimes Gracie Lynn Arrington wanted to kick off her goody-two shoes and just raise some hell. Unfortunately, it wouldn't be tonight. Not only because she was the maid of honor at her best friend's wedding reception, but also because it was hard to raise hell when you couldn't take a step without your walker. Although Frieda Mitchell seemed to be raising some hell with her walker. The eight-seven-year-old was doing the Cotton-eyed Joe with Old Man Sims, her feet shuffling much quicker than Gracie's could to the fast beat of the line dance.

"You want to give it a shot, Brat?"

She looked away from Frieda to find her brother Cole standing there looking as tall, dark, and handsome as ever in the white tux shirt and black pants. He looked just like his daddy while Gracie looked just like their mama. Cole could've hated her for that. But he didn't. He loved her, and she didn't know why after how she'd betrayed him.

"I think I'll pass," she said. "I'm stuffed after eating two slices of Ms. Marble's wedding cake. I couldn't decide on chocolate or strawberry. So I had both."

"Why, you little piglet." Cole reached out to ruffle her hair, something he'd done ever since she could remember, but then hesitated. "Emery says I need to stop doing that. She says women hate their hair messed." He glanced around and smiled slyly. "But since she's not here to get after me." He messed her hair.

Gracie laughed and slapped at his hand. "Where is Emery, anyway?"

Cole rolled his eyes. "Where else? She's at Aunt Lucy's gravesite."

Their great-aunt Lucy Arrington was the author of the classic western series Tender Heart. It was a set of ten fictional novels based on the mail-order brides who came to Bliss, Texas, in the late eighteen hundreds to wed the cowboys who worked the huge Arrington ranch. Lucy had died before writing the final book in the series . . . or so everyone had thought until Gracie stumbled upon a chapter in the little white chapel. That night had changed her life forever.

And not in a good way.

She smiled and tried not to show the fear that always accompanied any reminder of the accident. "She loves Lucy. She's probably just showing her respect."

Cole waved at Emmett Daily who owned the gas station where Cole was a mechanic. Cole didn't want to fix cars for a living. He wanted to breed horses. But in order to start his horse ranch, he needed money, something that had always been scarce in their family. "Or looking for the rest of that chapter," he said.

Gracie perked up. "The rest of what chapter?"

Cole turned to her, and his cheeks flushed a rosy pink. Blushing was the one physical trait he and Gracie had in common. They blushed when they were embarrassed . . . and when they were lying or trying to keep a secret.

Her heart rate picked up, and she squeezed Cole's arm in excitement. "Emery found another chapter while I was gone, didn't she? She was right. Lucy didn't just finish one chapter."

Cole glanced around before he shushed her. "Would you keep it down? Most the town is looking for that book after you found the first chapter. If word gets out we found another, there will be complete mayhem. Besides, Emery didn't find another chapter in the cemetery. She only found one page."

"But if she found one page, there has to be more." She went to reach for her walker, but Cole stopped her.

"This was exactly why I didn't mention finding the page. You don't think clearly when it comes to that book."

"But if we can find all the chapters, it will solve everything, Cole. It will pay off my hospital bills and the new stables for your horse ranch—"

He held up a hand. "Stop living in a fantasy world, Gracie. That book has been missing for fifty years and only one chapter and a page have been found. If Lucy finished the book, and that's a big if, the other chapters might not turn up for another fifty years. Which is why I'm thinking you should just sell the chapter that you found and be done with it."

Her eyes widened. "I could never do that, Cole. Lucy wanted that book published as a complete novel. I know in my heart that she did."

"You sound like Emery." He paused. "Although since we've been married she hasn't brought up the book much at all."

Gracie understood why. It was hard to discuss Tender Heart with a non-believer. And as much as she loved her brother, he was a non-believer. Tender Heart was just a fictional series to him, written by a selfish woman who hadn't left a dime of her royalties to her family. But she'd left the final book. Gracie was sure of it.

Something over her shoulder caught Cole's attention, and she didn't have to turn around to know who it was. His eyes filled with happiness and unconditional love. "I'll talk to you later, Brat," he said, and Gracie watched as he moved around the tables to the tent opening where Emery stood. He pulled her into his arms as if he couldn't wait to touch her.

The sight made Gracie feel happy and a little envious. What would it be like to have a man love you like that? Her gaze swept over the wedding guests, but the cowboy she searched for was nowhere in sight.

"Catch!"

The loudly spoken word caused her to swivel in her chair. Becky stood there, looking a little worse for wear. Her golden brown hair was falling out of its up-do and her mascara was smudged beneath her dark Arrington blue eyes. Eyes that twinkled with mischief as she drew back her arm and threw her bouquet like a slow-pitch softball. The flowers hit Gracie right in the chest before she caught them, sending pink rose petals to her lap.

She laughed. "What are you doing?"

Becky slipped into the chair next to her. "What does it look like I'm doing? I just tossed my bouquet."

Gracie rolled her eyes. "You can't toss it to only one person, Beck. You have to give all the single ladies a chance to catch it." She went to hand the bouquet back, but Becky refused to take it.

"I'm not tossing it for Winnie Crawley to catch. I couldn't live with myself if I helped saddle some poor guy with that woman." She smiled. "Besides, I want my favorite cousin to be next in line for a wedding."

Gracie set the bouquet on the table. "I don't think that's going to happen. Few men want to be stuck with a crip—"

Becky cut her off. "Don't you dare say it, Gracie Lynn. Not when you just got through walking down the aisle without one stumble."

"Only because I had a walker to hang onto."

Becky's chin turned stubborn. "Two months ago, you were in a wheelchair. I'd say that walking with a walker is a pretty big accomplishment. And in another month, I have no doubt that we can toss the walker like I did my bouquet."

Gracie wasn't so sure. She'd worked harder than all the other patients at the Dallas rehabilitation

center and her legs were still shaky and unde-
pendable. But before she could say anything about
her fears, Mason came and claimed his bride for
a dance.

He was as tall, dark, and handsome as Cole, but
a lot more serious. Gracie couldn't help but wonder how her vivacious cousin had fallen for such a
stoic man who liked to give orders.

He held out a hand. "Dance with me."

Becky ignored his hand and sent him a sassy
look. "I think you forgot the magic word."

Mason cocked an eyebrow, then smiled brighter
than Gracie had ever seen him smile. "Please,
Mrs. Granger."

The sassy look turned to one of adoration as
Becky took his hand and allowed him to pull her
to her feet. "I'm your servant, Mr. Granger." She
gave him a brief kiss before she turned to Gracie.
"Come on and dance with—"

A loud rumble cut her off, and all three of them
looked up. In fact, everyone in the tent stopped
what they were doing and looked at the tent ceiling. The music cut off as all the guests waited for
the next rumble. It came only a second later, followed by the splatter of raindrops on canvas.

"Yee-haws" filled the tent as the entire crowd
moved as one to the opening. It had been a hot,
dry summer. Rain was needed badly.

It took Gracie awhile to follow. She had been
sitting for too long and her leg muscles had tightened up. Even with the walker, her steps were
slow and unsteady. By the time she made it outside, rain was falling from the sky in sheets, and
the entire town was dancing around in celebra-

tion of the downpour.

She stood in the shelter of the tent and watched with a full heart. She'd missed her family and the people of Bliss more then she could ever put into words. This was the only home she'd ever known. The only place she ever wanted to live.

"Baby Girl!" Becky's brother Zane came out of the crowd and scooped her up his arms like she was a toddler, splattering her dress with the rain that dripped from his cowboy hat. Of course, a second later she had more than drips on her when he stepped out in the downpour and spun her around. Then she was passed to Cole who took a turn spinning before passing her to another town member who passed her to another. By the time she was set on her feet, she was soaked to the skin and completely out of breath from laughing.

She stood there for a few moments enjoying the celebration until her legs started to shake. She looked around for her brother or cousins, but they were all too wrapped up in the celebration to notice her. She glanced back at her walker. It was a good ten feet away. While she had walked that far without her walker, she had never done it without parallel bars to grab onto. Nor had she done it in a soaking wet maid-of-honor's dress that suddenly felt like it weighed a hundred pounds.

She took a deep breath and focused all her attention on taking a step. She had refused to wear the supportive running shoes her therapist had recommended, and instead wore pink cowboy boots that matched Becky's. The heels seemed to be glued to the wet ground, and it took all her strength to lift one foot. After only two steps, her muscles shook like leaves in a strong wind. She bit on her bottom lip and took another step. Unfortunately, the toe of her boot came down on the hem of her wet dress. The slight tug was all that was needed to send her sprawling to her hands and knees.

Humiliation welled up like the mud through her fingers. But before she could glance around to see who was watching, strong arms lifted her off the ground and cradled her against a hard chest. Her wet hair covered her face, but she didn't need to see to know who held her. Her body had grown a sensitivity to only one man.

"I got you, Miss Gracie."

The words spoken in the familiar deep, east Texas twang had her heart thumping in overtime and her cheeks burning with humiliation. She wanted to hide behind her hair forever, but she finally pushed it out of her face and looked at the man who held her.

Dirk Hadley had gotten even more handsome while she'd been away. He looked taller. His shoulders wider. And the biceps that flexed beneath his wet, transparent tuxedo shirt even bigger. The Texas summer sun had lightened his hair to golden honey and toasted his skin to a rich brown. The tan made his grayish-blue eyes look even grayer and his smile even whiter. He flashed that smile. And just like that, Gracie forgot to breathe.

She forgot a lot of things when Dirk smiled. Like how to talk.

"You okay, Miss Gracie?" he asked. "You need me to call for Cole? Or maybe the doc?"

She looked away from those mind-altering eyes and shook her head. "I'm more embarrassed than hurt." She noticed the mud she was getting on his white shirt and lifted her hand from his chest. "I'm getting you all dirty."

His arms tightened. "A little dirty never hurt anyone. And as for being embarrassed, there's no reason to be. All these yahoos are too busy celebrating to notice you taking a little spill."

But Dirk had noticed, the one person she didn't want seeing her wallowing around in the mud like a dressed-up sow. Another roll of thunder rumbled, and the rain fell in sheets from the darkening skies.

"We better get you out of this," Dirk said.

He carried her around the celebrating townsfolk to the little white chapel where Becky and Mason had just gotten married. It had been built in the late eighteen hundreds so the mail-order brides would have a respectable place to wed their cowboys. And for one brief moment, Gracie pretended that she was one of those brides. Not an original bride but her favorite fictional bride, Daisy McNeill. It wasn't a stretch to imagine Dirk as the charming Tender Heart hero, Johnny Earhart.

As he hurried through the rain, he bent his head so the brim of his cowboy hat shielded her head from the rain. With his face so close, she could see the darker burst of deep blue in his gray irises and feel the heat of his beer-scented breath on her lips.

Suddenly, she felt lightheaded and woozy as if she'd drank an entire six-pack of beer instead of two glasses of non-alcoholic punch. And when he shifted her to open the door, her arms tightened around his neck, her fingers accidentally brushing the heated skin beneath the crisp collar of his shirt. The contrast of her cold skin to his hot had him pausing and glancing down at her.

The smart thing to do would be to remove her hand and look away as if nothing had happened. Unfortunately, her mind was too immersed in her Tender Heart fantasy to be smart. It prompted her to do something stupid.

Something very, very stupid.

IF YOU ENJOYED
FALLING FOR A TEXAS HELLION,
BE SURE TO CHECK OUT THE OTHER BOOKS
IN KATIE LANE'S TENDER HEART TEXAS
SERIES!

Falling for Tender Heart

Falling Head Over Boots

And coming soon . . .
Falling for a Cowboy's Smile

OTHER SERIES BY KATIE LANE

ABOUT THE AUTHOR

KATIE LANE IS A USA Today Bestselling author of the *Deep in the Heart of Texas*, *Hunk for the Holidays*, *Overnight Billionaires*, and *Tender Heart Texas* series. She lives in Albuquerque, New Mexico, with her cute cairn terrier Roo and her even cuter husband Jimmy.

For more info about her writing life or just to chat, check out Katie on:

Facebook *www.facebook.com/katielaneauthor*
Twitter *www.twitter.com/katielanebook*
Instagram *www.instagram.com/katielanebooks*

.

And for upcoming releases and great give-aways, be sure to sign up for her mailing list at *www.katielanebooks.com*

Made in the USA
Middletown, DE
23 September 2017